THE LAST JOURNEY OF AGO YMERI

■ □ ■ □ ■

THE LAST JOURNEY OF AGO YMERI

BASHKIM SHEHU

Translated from the Albanian by
Diana Alqi Kristo

NORTHWESTERN UNIVERSITY PRESS

EVANSTON, ILLINOIS

Northwestern University Press
www.nupress.northwestern.edu

Copyright © 2007 by Northwestern University Press. Published 2007. All rights reserved.

Printed in the United States of America

10 9 8 7 6 5 4 3 2 1

ISBN-13: 978-0-8101-2110-2 (cloth)
ISBN-10: 0-8101-2110-7 (cloth)
ISBN-13: 978-0-8101-2111-9 (paper)
ISBN-10: 0-8101-2111-5 (paper)

Library of Congress Cataloging-in-Publication Data

Shehu, Bashkim.
  [Rrugëtimi i mbramë i Ago Ymerit. English]
  The last journey of Ago Ymeri / Bashkim Shehu ; translated from the Albanian by
Diana Alqi Kristo.
    p. cm. — (Writings from an unbound Europe)
  ISBN 978-0-8101-2111-9 (pbk. : alk. paper) — ISBN 978-0-8101-2110-2 (cloth : alk. paper)
  I. Kristo, Diana Alqi. II. Title. III. Series.
  PG9621.S453R7813   2007
  891.9913 — dc22
                                                                    2006039019

♾ The paper used in this publication meets the minimum requirements of the American
National Standard for Information Sciences — Permanence of Paper for Printed Library
Materials, ANSI Z39.48-1992.

When you come to the open meadows,
Look high and low for the ghostly shadows.

From an old song sung to the dead in the Albanian Northern Alps

■ □ ■ □ ■

THE LAST JOURNEY OF AGO YMERI

■ □ ■ □ ■

CHAPTER ONE

As if I were dreaming of huge, black waves, the very same waves that had engulfed me and where I was dissolving while dying . . .

WHEN SHE HAD NEARLY LOST ALL HOPE AND DECIDED SHE HAD BETTER go home, her eyes fell on a strange-looking man. Shivering in his bedraggled clothes, spotted most likely by the rain that had fallen throughout the previous night, with unkempt hair and a week's growth of beard on a ghastly pallid countenance, he stumbled forward, dragging his feet toward the village center at a sluggish, wobbly pace, occasionally raising his eyes toward the skies, scouring the rugged gray clouds in their mourning garb, as if in a vain search for the invisible sun. He must be a retard, thought the girl, but I'll talk to him anyway. After all I have nothing to lose. Wondering whether the stranger knew that she and her family were exiles, she approached him hesitantly, and her hesitation grew under the scrutiny of passersby and the vacant eyes of Mete the Blind, who as usual sat motionless at the foot of the huge oak tree right in the center of the square, listening as if in a trance to the rustling of the luxuriant foliage in the wind.

"Can you help me?" she asked the stranger, trying on her sweetest smile and, not pausing for a reply, adding: "Can you come with me as a witness . . . "

"A witness?" Still shivering, he threw an inquisitive look at her, while his forehead furrowed and wrinkled and his eyes narrowed as though delving into the meaning of that word.

"Not a witness in court," said the girl, her smile broadening slightly, "A witness, a best man in a marriage ceremony."

"Yes," the man said. "Sure, I can."

"Then would you wait here for us a little bit? I'm going to let my family know and we'll be back here in no time. Over there, there is my house . . . "

She pointed toward the village's only apartment house, which rose behind a handful of diminutive detached houses that girdled the square.

"All right, I'll wait here," he said.

"My sister is getting married," she added, for no apparent reason.

"My best wishes," he said, bestowing a smile upon her.

Mira ran off with a light gait and lighter spirits. At last, after wandering around the village for more than two hours with her friend Rita in search of a second witness for the ceremony, she had almost lost all hope, when lo and behold, she found him! There were four other banished families in the village but since one of them was the bridegroom's family, not one of its members could be used as a witness. All the other exiles, aside from Rita, were afraid of meddling in this affair, and so for days, conjuring up one excuse after the other, they all avoided them. Mira came out that morning hoping to find some other girl in the village, one of those girls who had shown some fondness toward her and who did not mind staying and talking with her, because you could find girls like that in this tiny isolated village. Most of the people she was looking for had already left for work, but even those few she met had either found a lame excuse, saying that they were busy, or they told her frankly that they could not come she must understand why and that she should not ask them such favors. Without a witness the ceremony would be postponed till next week, but even then finding a second witness would be most unlikely and the ceremony would again be put off for another week and then another and she thought this would go on forever. And the funniest thing was that the local authorities acted as if they had nothing to do with it, as if they behaved toward the exiled families exactly as they did toward everybody else, but it was the fear the authorities infused in one thousand and one ways that created the impenetrable void that surrounded the exiles and thwarted everything. At last Mira found this weirdo, a living scarecrow, who had emerged from God knows where, from a fairy tale or from the world of ghosts, solely to help them. The closer she came to her house the more anxious she became lest her father, morose and difficult as he was, would scold her for finding such a character and for making an immature and unacceptable decision.

Her father did reproach her but for quite another reason.

"How dare you leave him outside," he snapped. "Why didn't you invite him in?"

"I . . . I forgot," she murmured. "I was in a hurry."

The idea of bringing him in had never crossed her mind. The stranger should never know they were banished, and the best thing to do was to keep him at arm's length and talk to him as little as possible. Otherwise, she told herself, if he learned about it, he would hardly deign to accept. Oh, somebody else, one of those who saw her at the square, could tell him about her family. She felt guilty for telling the stranger an innocent white lie. But it was too late for any remedies. Her sister was ready by now, as was the groom, who lived in the same apartment building since he too was an exile. Thus, the preparations for the ceremony had already started and could not be reversed.

In no time a bizarre group of people—the bridegroom, the bride, two girls, and the bedraggled stranger—walked through the village to the town hall. Mira walked beside the stranger. The sullen gazes of the townspeople made her seek some kind of solace in the stranger, and right away she felt a touch of closeness toward him, something like trust.

"I have to tell you something . . . something I forgot to mention to you . . . We are exiles," Mira blurted, not really knowing how she managed it.

Her sister threw her a bewildered and angry look, whereas the stranger only shook his head as if he already knew or at least had assumed, but perhaps he had not understood what she said at all.

In the town hall the service was conducted in haste. When the time came for the stranger to sign, he stood there transfixed, with his eyes glued upon the date on the paper, looking as if he didn't know what to do. Everybody assumed he was illiterate. Then he took the pen and scribbled what seemed to be a signature.

Soon after, they and the stranger were back home.

"Where are you from?" asked the master of the house.

"From Tirana," the stranger said.

"What good fortune brought you here?" asked another older man, the bride's uncle. "Are you, God forbid, in the same plight as we?"

"No, I'm not banished," the stranger said. "I was in one of those villages by the coast, beyond those hills." He waved vaguely. "I stayed with some relatives. I got lost on my way back."

"Go, fetch some clean clothes for him," the master of the house ordered.

"I set the copper on the fire early this morning," his wife added. "The water must be ready by now."

"The water is hot," said Mira, who had just stepped in from the adjacent room.

"You may take a bath," urged the mistress. "You are the guest of the house. Consider yourself at home." Then she turned to her daughter, "Bring him some of your brother's clothes."

He followed Mira's steps through the hallway onto the patio outside. He threw a quizzical look at her.

"You know what?" the girl said with a playful smile as if trying to hide her bashfulness. "The copper is upstairs on the terrace and I cannot carry it all by myself. Can you help me? It is not that heavy . . . "

"Sure, let's go," he said.

"What's your name?" she asked as they climbed the stairs.

"Viktor," he said after a moment, and then he spoke again, "My name is Viktor Dragoti."

The girl thought he pronounced his name as if he were sure it would ring a bell. She was sure she had never heard his name before.

They came out onto the terrace. He raised his eyes and for a moment he stared at the bleak dome of the sky.

"Here it is," Mira said, pointing at the steaming black copper supported by half bricks placed around the fire. Just as the wind began to blow out the fire, it rekindled and started again.

His gaze had drifted off over the mist-covered plains and seemed somehow voracious.

"Are you coming from the penitentiary?" Mira asked.

"Well . . . yes and no," the stranger said, and he pursed his lips into a smile at last.

"You are so strange," Mira said.

"You are a strange girl, too . . . "

"Listen, I have a brother who is in the penitentiary," she said, and her smile faded. "These clothes are his. I think they'll fit you perfectly."

"May God help him come home soon . . . "

Holding the copper by the handles, they brought it slowly down the stairs and into the house.

After he bathed and changed, Viktor came back to the room where the others had already gathered. Helped by her two daughters, the mistress of the house was serving raki and some entrées. Toasts were raised to the health of the bride and groom and in honor of the guest. Then in low, muffled tones the elderly guests began to sing a wedding song. It rose from abysmal depths, making for the skies, other depths but this time of light, in which joy and sorrow were intermingled. And there was something pitiful and contorted in this celebration, in which only the elderly sang as the young listened in silence. Mira was not paying much attention to the song. Her mind had drifted somewhere else, and time and again she cast fleeting glances at the guest. Now he was transformed and had become a different man. He looked younger, most likely in his thirties, and yet there was something in him that drew her attention. Perhaps it was his rather unusual appearance, or maybe his clothes. The clothes all the others were wearing, the best they had for this special occasion, were worn out by time, while those of the guest were fairly well preserved, still new and quite different from the clothes she had seen in this forlorn place during the long years of their banishment. The stranger's clothes reminded her of another world that once was hers too and which she longed for. Or perhaps the look of this man, his posture and his gaze, made the clothes look better. It dawned upon her that she yearned for this man. And because she yearned for him, there must be something about him. She would like to make love to him. She had never felt this urge for any other male, at least not like this. She had been young, under sixteen, when they banished and confined her family here, and now she was over twenty and had never experienced love. She felt intuitively that making love would be something terribly wondrous, sweet, and painful, and yet she had never allowed herself to venture it. As an exile, surrounded by scorn, she learned to look at the world with scorn, and the thought of giving herself like that to someone was too demeaning. The thought of it was almost a punishment she inflicted upon herself. Her skin had started to lose its luster. The sun, dust, and frost were taking their toll, and her body was suffering the untimely consequences of hard labor. Still she felt she had not completely lost her feminine attraction, and, if she chose, she could stop punishing herself. Aware of that, she felt more at ease. A nun. You are a nun, her close friend Rita teased. Some time ago Rita had found a soldier from Tirana whom she met in secret somewhere down by the brook. I allowed him to do everything with me, she once confided to Mira. It was the first time she had discovered the pleasures of indulging in men and she said it was the most wonderful thing in the world, the greatest pleasure ever to be offered to humans, and she prattled on and on. Then the young man was released from the army and she never saw him again. Rita was not sorry for what had happened. On the contrary, whenever she thought of it she was overwhelmed with happiness. Mira was different. She could never do what Rita had done. Even so she did not feel contempt for what her friend had done and could not reproach her. Deep down she knew her friend was right. At night she dreamed the same dream over and over again. In this dream, she saw herself going to work, all alone, and somewhere along a forgotten path a stranger came out of the bushes, or rather an unidentified male but always the same one nonetheless, and threw her to the ground, always with the same brutality, tore off her clothes and took from her forcibly what she did not want to give him willingly, and she liked it. And then quite unexpectedly she shivered from head to toe because at last she realized the man who raped her in her dream was the man she had met in the morning and who was now sitting opposite her. Remembering the presence of the others and the morose look of her father, she hurriedly suppressed her startling realization.

In the meantime the elderly guests had sung two or three more songs so similar they seemed to be the same song. Then they started to talk with one another. As a sign of respect they tried to engage the guest in conversation, but whenever they unintentionally mentioned the predicament that had befallen them, they carefully let the flow of the conversation drift in another direction. During the conversation, the guest occasionally threw a fleeting glance at the guitar hanging in a corner on the wall.

The master of the house followed his glance and said, "Would you like to play it? It belongs to my son. My son is locked up there, in that terrible place. I wouldn't wish that even on my enemy. It's been five years now and no one knows how many more."

"He'll be back. He'll be back sooner than you expect," the guest said.

"Bless you," the old man said. "His is a very complicated case. He committed a grave crime, he meddled with politics."

The other smiled a bitter smile.

"Nevertheless, he'll be back soon," he added.

Those present stood there in bewilderment, in a state between fear and hope, a vague frail hope, overwhelmed by fear.

"Would you like to play it?" the host asked, changing the subject.

"Yes," the guest said. Mira unhooked the guitar from the wall and handed it over to him.

"I'd like to sing a song in honor of the bride and the groom. It is a song dedicated to a loyalty that withstands the most ruthless twists and turns of fate. It is as old as the world itself and yet ever so young."

After striking two or three chords, he turned to the bride and groom. "May your destiny bear a lifetime of happiness and none of the evil you'll hear me sing about in this song."

He paused for a moment as the others looked at him in silence, holding their breath. Then he started to sing. The song was more of a melodious recitative, accompanied by the guitar in arpeggios. It was gentle and drawling whereas his voice resounded reverberatingly. The master of the house, apparently scared, signaled to him to keep it down. Viktor lowered his voice and the song poured more tranquilly, smoothly, and softly, and yet in its softness there was an erosive perseverance. A new song reverberated from within the old as if from within a swirling whirlpool. At first Mira could not concentrate and could not get into the meaning of its words, only sensing that sometime, somewhere she had heard this song before. Gradually she realized that this melodious recitative was a version of the old legend of Ago Ymeri, though the Ago Ymeri of this song was not a prisoner in a strange land, he was dead and in the underworld, where the shadows of the dead wander. The character Ago Ymeri addressed was neither a king nor a queen of distant foreign realms but the god of

9

the underworld himself, and Ago Ymeri pleaded that he be permitted to return to the living and meet with his true love one last time. The heart of the god of the underworld mellowed in the face of Ago Ymeri's earnest pleading. Mira had heard somewhere, most likely in school, that the legend of Ago Ymeri originated from *The Odyssey,* which she still remembered vividly though she had read it ages ago. The music of the song sounded so outlandish, almost unknown to her, and yet she perceived a faint resemblance to the songs of those young singers she had heard back in Tirana, in the private quarters of some of her sister's friends. Back then it was whispered those songs were banned. This memory made her shiver with fear. Viktor's singing suddenly seemed dangerous to her, but despite this, or perhaps because of it, she decided to give herself to this man that very same day. No doubt he would accept the invitation to stay for the night, she thought, so that he could attend the modest wedding dinner the next day.

After the sound of the last stroke died down and he laid the guitar aside, all were still speechless with awe.

"Well, now, I apologize but I must leave. I have a long way to go . . . "

As if released from a spell, the people in the room started to talk to him all at once, inviting him to stay as he tried to explain to them that he could not stay any longer.

"We're going to celebrate tomorrow, we're having a modest dinner," the groom's father insisted. "Aren't you coming to see us too? You must come . . . "

"I have a long way to go," the guest repeated. "I'd like to stay but I have to go to Tirana. I'm already late, I have to hurry."

He's going to see his girlfriend no doubt, said Mira to herself. Who is this Penelope who waits for you? Mira-Nausicaa, still enchanted by the presentation of the song, by that dream in verse, felt that another woman was taking him away from her forever.

The other people in the room realized at last that the guest could not stay. Some food was prepared for him to take on his journey, and he rose to go.

"You brought us good luck," they told him as they escorted him to the door. "May favorable winds steer you wherever you go and may you have the best of luck!"

Mira's eyes followed him as he disappeared over the horizon and realized she felt relieved that the man would not come into her life. Her wandering eyes fell on a few people who were staring at her, and in an attempt to avert her eyes, she caught a glimpse of Mete the Blind, who, as always, was sitting at his preferred place at the foot of the huge oak tree, whose dark foliage was exchanging arcane signals with the skies.

■ □ ■ □ ■

CHAPTER TWO

Nobody blinded me . . .

HMM, BITCH, GRUNTED QEMAL, STRIDING TO AND FRO IN HIS OFFICE. His office, one of the empty apartments at the disposal of the Sigurimi, used only when he or his fellow workers came to the village, was located on the first floor of the apartment building where the exiles lived. Mira lived there too, and he had sent someone to summon her quite a while ago but she had not come yet. Qemal was losing his temper. Who knows where the whore is meandering now, he thought. That morning he woke up with the idea that he should insist she become his. He had hinted at it several times in the past but had never had the guts to put it bluntly to her and did not know why. It is not that he hesitated or got confused or was too diffident to do so. Quite the contrary. Whenever he summoned her he felt his self-confidence grow stronger, just as it did when he talked to all the outcasts, and he felt that way as he conversed with her, until the moment he had to say that word, that little word he had thought of saying hundreds of times. At that very moment he faltered, withdrew into himself while the conversation still hung on in loops, and the young woman pretended she did not understand anything about his advances, or perhaps she really did not understand, or it never crossed her mind. No, no way. It was impossible for her not to understand him. But the language he was using was vague and ambiguous, leaving her a loophole, letting her get to another meaning, and he was left with only her icy derision. He must talk to her more explicitly and let her know outright she had no way of escaping and, willingly or unwillingly, she must give in. After all, she was to some extent at his mercy. But he held back as if scared of her. Were he to make such advances she might complain about him to his superiors. But on the other hand, he reasoned, he could fire back and explain to them that this banished woman, the enemy, was making up things against the Sigurimi agents to tarnish the people's power. It was her way of revenge to bring as much harm as possible to this power. She could do no greater harm than this. And while his words would undoubtedly carry more weight, there existed the danger of her words taking root somewhere. Even so she would be the one to suffer the gravest consequences. On the other hand, to make it clear to her he had to say it, and to do so he had to tell her first about that other thing, which he had not succeeded in doing yet. He was apprehensive of her. It was a kind of apprehension he realized quite vaguely, lest her icy derision, dormant so far, would pour over him and chill everything forever. By bandying about equivocal and enigmatic expressions, by beating about the bush, he could continue this kind of foreplay forever. Qemal liked it and, more and more often in the course of conversation, he felt almost as if he were possessing her, and the satisfaction he derived from this anticipation was similar to the overwhelming contentment of carnal pleasure. It was this sensation that had driven him once to pursue carnal pleasure to the end. When he was working as an investigator about three years ago, he had the chance to interrogate a prostitute who gave herself to him without hesitation. Mira was a prostitute, but she was different from the other one in that Mira was more desirable. Mira was a whore all right, but she was also an enemy, and besides, she was the type who did not give up easily. Just when he thought he would have her in his possession, she slithered, writhed into herself. This was not a sign of girlish chastity, but of that icy derision with which she overcame her fear. Again and again he felt sure that he would make her his own, that he would possess her in no time, but he always became afraid lest from the cracks and fissures of her defenses a torrent of ridicule and scorn would pour forth and overwhelm him. Yet he thought he was closing in on his prey. That morning, while still in bed, he had decided to go to her village, which was under his jurisdiction, and reveal his intentions to her outright. But when he came to the village, his informants reported a few things that threatened to shatter all his plans. Initially, when they told him she had met a man, a bedraggled stranger, he felt confused, and then a bitter twinge, as if a serpent had bit him, poisoned his blood and stirred his soul. She's found her beau, he thought, noticing that he had become jealous and hating himself for that. Jealous of whom, of that whore, the enemy, the bitch in heat who's ready to follow any stray dog that stumbles her way? But then he started to enjoy the idea that this bitch would go straight for any dog. Since you are willing to go with that scoundrel, here I am at least a hundred times better, Qemal addressed her in his mind. Nonetheless, he could not decide whether to interrogate Mira about the stranger or deal with the other thing. The appearance of the stranger could foil his plans for Mira because now he had to interrogate her at length about him, the more so since the stranger had vanished into thin air, which was quite suspicious. And yet he needed courage to say what he needed to say to Mira, where could he again find that daredevil courage that was provided by the occasion of today's interrogation? He could start by asking her about the stranger and then steer her into his trap, but in the meantime some very important piece of information might come up and he would have to perform his duties, and as a result he would not be able to talk about the other thing he had thought of a thousand times, even this morning. Consequently, either one or the other. This unresolved shilly-shallying, this ebb and flow, made his nerves on edge and the longer it took her to report in, the more irresolute he became.

At last he heard a knock on the door.

"Come in," Qemal barked.

The door opened slightly and a head popped in. It was Shezai, his deputy resident informant.

"What the hell do you want?" Qemal shouted at him.

"With your permission, Chief," stammered the other.

"Come in. Speak up. What is it you want to tell me?"

"I went to the town hall and I saw the records myself, with my own eyes," Shezai said. "The name of one of the witnesses was not there, it was not taken down, his signature was illegible."

"Really? Hell . . . irresponsible people."

"Yes, sir."

Qemal paced his office as Shezai followed his movements, scared stiff.

"Why are you looking at me like that," Qemal said. "Aren't you gone yet?"

"I have more, Chief. They informed me . . . besides the stranger dressed as a beggar, another stranger went to see the Gjonaj family today."

"Is that so?" Qemal said, making an abrupt turn. "Is he still there or has he already left?"

"Yes, he left about an hour ago in the direction of Malas . . . "

"What was he like? Can you describe him to me?"

"He was tall, not very tall . . . thin, what can I say . . . he had black hair like this," and he raised his hand to his head in an effort to describe what he could not with words.

"How was he dressed?"

"Dressed? Citylike. Tight, fitted clothes just like the people in the city . . . dark jacket and dark pants, I can't say black . . . they weren't the same color. Would you like to talk to the individual who saw him?"

"Shut up! Get the hell out of here!"

Shezai scurried out. Qemal remained alone. It must be him, he thought, as he resumed pacing the room. On his way to the village, as he was walking along the other side of the brook, having barely reached the wooden bridge, Qemal had come across a man he had never seen before in that area, yet for a fleeting moment he'd thought he recognized that face and almost exchanged greetings with him. Nevertheless that morning he was in too great a hurry and too overwhelmed by lust to pay any attention to anybody, and consequently he had almost forgotten him then and there. Even if he'd known what had happened in the village, what could he have done? Accordingly, he had to interrogate Mira first, then the others, each in turn. Hmm, the appearance of a second stranger complicated matters further. His boss was completely wrong to have ordered the removal of the listening devices from the Gjonajs' apartment. Qemal would have learned a lot more if they had still been in there. The removal happened after five years of silence and infuriating small talk that was worse than silence. The Gjonajs had acted as though scared and mindful only of their own business. After being appointed to that location, Qemal would often go there and stay awake on his cot till daybreak, his head between the earphones, monitoring and monitoring all night through. He came to recognize her breathing. In her sleep her breathing became heavier, more tangible, especially during the hot summer nights, as her chest heaved painfully and her full breasts, sagging a little but still firm, were almost bursting out of her tight nightgown, and the shadow between her breasts enticed him to plunge his face ravenously within and lose himself in her breathing, which resounded in his head, pressed between the two earphones as if between her firm breasts. But his boss deprived him of that pleasure last summer. The night they debugged, Qemal stayed there in the apartment, and though he did not have the earphones, he could picture more clearly than ever before how her bare shoulder and then her bare waist showed in the dark, that night it was so hot one could not even lie between the sheets, and then her naked hips, she was not wearing anything that night, and all her other private parts, dazzling white for never having been exposed to the sun, and his hand went instinctively down to his groin and fondled feverishly until he felt it become wet. Afterward he was embarrassed. And maybe because of that he could not sleep in the Sigurimi apartment any longer. Nevertheless he still continued to summon the young woman as if it were his job to do so, and he dragged his equivocal conversation on and on, and in so doing he felt calm and confident and yet his insatiable desire made him summon her more and more often, again and again. He must set a limit, he should be more prudent and not arouse any suspicion. He should not drag it out forever. He must make her his own as soon as possible and at all cost.

His brooding was interrupted by a knock on the door.

"Come in," Qemal yelled, rather startled.

This time it was she. She threw him a cold glance.

"You did not deign to come when we called you," Qemal spoke again.

"They just called me and here I am," said Mira. "What is it you want?"

"Take a seat . . . sit down. How are you?"

"Not bad," said the girl, sitting down.

"Why do you say 'not bad'? Oh, because you are banished. It depends on your behavior and your attitude if you want to be released from banishment . . . "

"Why did you call me?" Mira asked again.

"Hmm," said Qemal. "You know very well why I called you."

He fixed his devouring beady eye on her while she, entrapped, could not take her eyes from his other eye, the glass one. The misty derision that masked her trepidation started to dissipate. He felt her withdrawal. I got you, Medusa, he said to himself. Her scintillating tear-filled eyes seemed more beautiful, more winning in her weathered face. Plunging deep into her eyes, his single eye could grasp a flutter of angst in them, the quivering of an unprotected small animal. And his single eye started to strip her of her clothes. Oh, no, hold on, he told himself, it is still too soon to attack, you have to wait.

"Is there anything new?" he said out loud with a certain nonchalance, and to make it more visible, he took a pencil from the table and started to play with it, twisting it round his fingers.

"Nothing," said the girl, forcing a smile.

The bewilderment she felt at the beginning had worn off. Hmm, she's used to this by now, Qemal thought. It is my fault, always the same thing. No, today it is different, I'll show her.

"Are you sure?" Qemal spoke out.

"Nothing," repeated the girl.

"Whom did you meet with today?" he said rather indifferently, as if his mind were engaged with something else.

"Is this why you called me today?" the girl fired back. "I can meet with anybody I like and I do not have to render an account to anybody for it."

She rose and made for the door, but Qemal waved at her to stop.

"Wait, hold on. You can meet with anybody you like but it is not as simple as it may seem. Do you think I ask you these questions just for fun?"

The girl sat down obediently. She was not as calm and self-contained as she tried to appear. Her earlier aggravation showed and she felt vulnerable, realizing that he knew she was hiding something from him. She could not escape his single eye, which was more penetrating than a thousand eyes taken together. Her icy derision was wearing off again. I got you, Medusa, I got you, he shouted to himself. His glass eye, a lonely hungry leech, sucked at her gaze furiously while he imagined her Medusa's tentacles, which were both the unprotected little beast and the relentless hunter at the same time, sweeping over his body and caressing his groin, giving him frenzied pleasure. Aroused, he thought it was the right moment to conquer her, to make her his. But he stood stock-still, then abruptly poured out all the words he had saved for this moment.

"Tell me, who were the two strangers you met with?"

"I met with only one stranger," Mira snapped.

See how she is writhing, the bitch. Wait, I'll show you. "Probably neither of those you met was unknown to you," he said, reaching for the pencil again and twisting it between his fingers. "I mean those two who were not from this village and who have not been seen here before."

For a moment Mira staggered in confusion. "It was only one," she said. "I had not seen him before. I met him quite by chance, at the village square . . . "

"What was he like? Can you describe him to me?"

"He was very poorly dressed and looked like he spent most of his life in the woods."

"Are you related to him in any way? Why did he come to your house?"

"Why did he come to our house?" Mira repeated in an effort to pull herself together. "This is what happened. I asked him to come as a witness to my sister's wedding ceremony, since we could not find anybody else. Then we invited him home. Is there anything bad in this? Do we have to ask for permission when we invite somebody over?"

It is important that she is talking, Qemal thought, even though she is trying to justify herself. At least she feels compelled to respond.

"Well, this I know," he said out loud. "What else?"

"Else? I gave him some clothes and then he left. Is there anything bad in this? Do we have to ask permission even for that?"

Now Qemal felt somewhat confused. There was something in this that was not quite right.

"What about the other individual?" he said.

"Who?" asked Mira.

"The other one, the one who came to your house an hour and a half or two hours ago . . . "

"There is no other one," Mira said. "It was one and the same person." Her lips twisted in a sardonic grin.

Hmm, thought Qemal for a moment, this is it.

"What's his name?" he asked again.

Mira hesitated, then said, "Viktor."

Bitch, you are lying, Qemal said to himself.

"Viktor who?"

"I don't know," Mira replied.

You are still lying, you bitch. Just give me a second. He felt the desire rising within him as he continued to question her.

"What else do you know about him?"

"We did not interrogate him as you are doing to me," Mira said, and her lips drew back again in a scornful grin.

Qemal kept quiet for a while as if to gather his strength and measure it prior to the final attack. He started to scrutinize her again. She thinks she's safe now and yet she's wondering why I'm not letting her go, and why I'm looking at her like this, and why I've stopped talking.

"Don't you know he is a subversive agent?!" he snarled, irritated at last, rendering her speechless. "You gave shelter to a subversive agent. You collaborated with him. You helped him disguise himself."

"We did not know anything," she tried to justify herself.

"Is that so?" Qemal grimaced. "Where did he go then?"

"He left for Tirana," the girl said.

"Is that so? Well, you can go now," Qemal said, and as she made for the door he added, "Listen, if I find out that you knew who he was and what he was, you'll suffer the consequences."

"We did not know anything," Mira said, terrified.

She went out.

Now she'll feel restless and anxious till I call her next time, he said to himself. Then I'll have all the time in the world to talk to her at leisure.

As for now, he had no time to lose, not even to call other family members and interrogate them about the subversive agent. He was already pretty confident the stranger was a subversive agent because how else could he explain Mira's restlessness when she was questioned about him. He decided to pursue the stranger without further delay. He needed to find him before he could get out of his area of jurisdiction, or at least the district, and Qemal could not let him reach Tirana by any means. He had to hurry.

A few minutes later, the cooperative chairman's Gaz 69 was heading toward Tirana with Qemal on board. The chauffeur was driving fast. They caught up with several trucks heading in the same direction, and after halting them Qemal asked the passengers for their IDs. None of them was the one Qemal was looking for. At least, no one appeared to bear any resemblance. He regretted that he had not brought along the informant who had seen the man. By and by he calmed down, reasoning that the stranger might have taken the bus. They caught up with the bus near the small town that was the center of the municipality.

"Slow down," Qemal ordered the chauffeur. "Don't pass it. Just follow it."

The bus made a long stop in that town so that the passengers could get out and find lunch because they had a long way to travel yet. Qemal thought he'd better wait for the stranger to get off the bus. This would enable him to best survey him without being noticed and then find the appropriate moment to apprehend him. He would try to do so without asking for his ID.

"Pull over there," he said to the chauffeur, as the bus was reaching the station.

Qemal jumped out of the car and approached the bus at a distance, casually watching the people as they got off. And there he was, the stranger he was looking for, he could recognize him among other passengers. It was the same man he'd come across that morning on his way to the village, and again he got the impression that he had seen him somewhere before. He started to walk nonchalantly in his direction. Falling in alongside the stranger, Qemal reached in his pocket and produced a cigarette. "Please, Comrade, do you have a light?"

"I'm sorry, I don't," the stranger responded promptly, and then, surprised, he burst out, "Oh, Qemal, is that you?"

Qemal stood there flabbergasted, his mouth half-open and the cigarette stuck on his lower lip. There facing him stood Viktor Dragoti, his former classmate from first grade through senior high. Qemal recognized him, of course it was him. But Viktor Dragoti was dead and gone for nine years. And yet, this was Viktor Dragoti and no one else, Qemal told himself. It was the same face, which surprisingly enough had not changed, and the same voice he could never mistake for someone else's. He could not, however, question the report of the Ministry of the Interior to all the Sigurimi employees regarding the coast guard's killing of Viktor Dragoti as he attempted to cross the border. Either I have gone crazy or resurrection from the dead is true, he said to himself. But the other man took no notice of Qemal's bewilderment. He decided to fake recognition since Viktor could not know Qemal was now working for the Sigurimi. And thus, he reasoned, during the conversation with Viktor he could collect as much information from him as possible without him having the slightest doubt as to the reason for his questions. While Qemal still could not work out a reason that he would be questioning Viktor as part of his job duties, there was something gnawing at him from within, a kind of presentiment that it was precisely his job to deal with this.

"Hey, Viktor. How are you?" he roared at last, extending his arm irresolutely between a proffered handshake and an embrace. The stranger enfolded him in his arms and Qemal hugged him back.

"How are you, Qemal? How is everything going with you?"

"You vanished into thin air, Viktor, my pal, I haven't seen you for ages. How are you? How are things going with you?"

"Okay, all right . . . How about you?"

"Not bad . . . Do you have some time to sit together and have a little chitchat? How about it?"

"Yes, sure." Viktor said. "I have another twenty minutes before the bus leaves."

"Half an hour?" Qemal said. "You know what, let's go to a restaurant, it's lunchtime already."

The restaurant was located adjacent to the bus station. At last they found a free table and ordered the only dish the restaurant had. Viktor had some food with him, and he unwrapped it on the table. Qemal ordered a bottle of wine. The drink would make him more garrulous, Qemal thought.

"Where are you coming from?" he said aloud.

"Where I come from," Viktor said and his eyes dimmed as he forced a smile. "I come from afar, from very, very far away . . . "

Hmm, from very, very far away. Qemal dwelled upon the words. Is he a subversive agent? What if he wasn't killed and has infiltrated now as a subversive agent, sent by an alien country? No, no way, this can never happen, the Party never lies, he thought and instantaneously felt scared of his own presumption. Nonetheless he drew closer to Viktor and whispered so that no one sitting at the nearby tables could overhear him, "Viktor, I thought you were dead."

Viktor's forehead furrowed painfully and for a moment he stood there speechless. For a second time Qemal caught himself funneling the conversation in a direction that made the other man look the subversive agent and himself the pursuer, though on the other hand, he was positive Viktor was not an agent. What is happening to me? he shrieked inwardly. Meanwhile, he felt Viktor's gaze on his glass eye. This reminded him of Mira and immediately he felt somewhat elated, becoming once again conscious of his power, something that happened to him whenever he felt ill at ease conversing with someone. And he set about scrutinizing Viktor with his other eye.

"It's true, I'm dead," Viktor calmly broke the silence at last, as if he were pronouncing the most common words.

"What, dead!" Qemal said, hardly restraining himself from screaming. "What I can see is that you are alive! You see, hear, speak, eat just as I do. So it means you are alive!"

"I come from the world of the dead," Viktor said slowly, with the same calmness, "I come from there."

"How is it possible?" Qemal said, full of curiosity now. "Come, come, tell me. How could you come back from there?"

Viktor's forehead was again clouded by deep furrows.

"I don't know," he said after a pause. "I don't remember. I remember something as if in a dream. As if I were dreaming of huge, black waves, the very same waves that had engulfed me and where I was dissolving while dying and then being resurrected from the same waves that swirled me in their dark interior and I felt as if I was awakening and coming out of a dream and yet I stayed within the dream, which was the inside of a huge black wave that kept swirling and which was concurrently inside me until I found myself tossed on the sand, somewhere on the coast . . . "

At this point Viktor was not staring at the glass eye, but at the other, the live one. Qemal struggled to penetrate his interlocutor with his single eye, infuse anxiety into him, make him recede into himself, render him powerless to protect himself in front of his might, but he failed, and he felt his sound eye gradually start to die out and turn to glass.

"And now, where are you going?" Qemal said, in a last-ditch attempt to change the subject of their conversation.

"To Tirana," Viktor replied.

Qemal believed everything the other told him, yet he wondered how he could believe him and hunt him down simultaneously. He had to, there was no other choice, though he did not understand why he had to do that and what he would try to make out of it. Now he felt terribly confused. He drank the glass of wine to the last drop and filled it a second time. Viktor hardly took a sip.

"How was it like there, in the other world?" Qemal asked, urged by a blind impulse to ask him over and over again, without knowing where that would lead.

Viktor shook his head and his face contorted spasmodically. Qemal raised his glass again as if to give him some time, but Viktor did not utter a word.

"I apologize," Qemal said. "I did not intend to hurt you by reminding you of bitter experiences . . . I can imagine how bad it is. Or probably it is impossible to imagine how bad it is unless you've been there . . . However, it is amazing you have not changed at all in the last nine years since you were down there. You have remained so young . . ."

"Nine days," Viktor butted in. "Not nine years."

"Nine years," Qemal insisted.

"No way!"

"You don't believe it?" Qemal took a newspaper out of his pocket. "Look at this . . ."

Viktor took the newspaper, brought it close, and strained his eyes as if he could not see well.

"October 15, 1976! Well, you see now?"

"You are right," Viktor said. "I saw the date somewhere else, on an official document in a registrar's office where I was brought by some people who wanted me to become a witness in a marriage ceremony. But I thought the date was wrong."

He paused for an instant and then, as though submerged in his own thoughts, added, "And yet only nine days passed down there, that is, today is the ninth day. To tell you the truth you could see neither sun nor moon there, only a dome of dense darkness covering everything as in eternal black anguish. However, you could figure out time, and there were only nine days . . ."

Qemal was listening to him in awe. A far-off memory of his early childhood flashed in his brain, which was shrouded in the fumes of his drink, a tale his grandmother had told him about how time flows differently in the world of the dead, it flows slowly, far too slowly, one year compares to thousands of years among the living.

"I have to go now," Viktor said as if shaking himself awake, showing signs of edginess.

"Hold on, you can't leave like this," Qemal said almost imploringly.

"I'm pressed for time," Viktor said. "Good-bye."

And he scurried past the tables to the door and out into the street, while Qemal remained behind in stunned amazement, not knowing what to do. To follow him would be futile. What else could he learn from him? Yet he had to do something. He had to report to his superiors. But what was he to report to them? How could he explain the idea of resurrection? He could not keep it to himself, though. This concerned Viktor Dragoti, an enemy, a traitor who had tried to defect abroad, and this made it imperative for him to report his presence without delay. Yet, Viktor had died nine years ago, and this complicated everything. First he thought he would track him down, arrest him, and then escort him by force if need be to the district branch of the Ministry of the Interior. But what if this move made matters worse? By arresting him now, the Sigurimi would not have a chance to discover through surveillance this traitor's contacts and for what possible reason he had returned. Because he must have a mission, there must be a reason for his return, and what was more, he had even returned from the underworld. That last fact made it impossible for Qemal to guess the purpose of his return. So, how could Viktor's mission be divulged if he were to proceed with the arrest right away? Better let him loose and then report the case to his superiors. However reasonable this solution seemed, his overloaded mind could find no way of breaking the news to his superiors, which left him right back at the starting point, not knowing what to do and where to turn. Oh, my mind is going berserk, he said to himself. Qemal gulped down another glass of wine, which made him more daring. Come what may, he decided to inform the chief in person and let him untie the knot.

Qemal left money on the table and dashed outside, as if running for his life, through the streets to the police station. The door of the station was locked. The chief must have gone to his village, today being Saturday, said Qemal to himself, and his subordinates are treating his absence as a holiday, kicking up their heels and frolicking. He left the station annoyed and disillusioned and went in search of an officer who might be patrolling the streets. A little farther down the street his eyes fell on the decrepit post office building and it occurred to him that it would be a good idea to make a phone call from there. En avant!

Though there were few people in the post office, the telephone booth—the only one there—was occupied. He waited behind the glass door for what seemed a long time. A stout middle-aged woman inside the booth kept on talking and seemed to have no intention of stopping. Qemal was losing his patience. Not knowing what else to do, with no precise intention in mind, he started prying into the conversation. Through the glass door of the booth, he could discern a few words here and there, mostly numbers, one-digit figures, which once put together could result in multiple-digit numbers of various combinations that very well might be a secret code, the more so because the woman seemed very much angst-ridden and frantic, so he became all ears, pressing his face to the glass so as not to miss a word. But the woman was rambling on and on and only occasionally raising her voice enough for him to hear, therefore he did not wait any longer but made for the console area and whispered a few words to the operator, who handed him a headset. Now he could monitor what the lady in the booth and the lady on the other end of the line were saying, and he came to understand that the numbers were card numbers and their conversation was about fortune-telling, and a very skilled fortune-teller was explaining to the lady on this end her fortune, but probably this fortune-telling-and-card thing was just a way to disguise the code better, the code of an underground espionage network. Here it was, another job for him. But he had no time to figure out whether telephone fortune-telling and secret codes would fall under his jurisdiction because the stout woman came out of the booth and he had to dash inside because he had that other very urgent job to tackle.

Qemal was connected to the branch chief and briefed him, trying all the time to be as explicit as possible.

"Where are you now?" He could distinguish the concern in the chief's voice on the other end of the line.

"I'm calling you from the post office," Qemal said.

"Stay there, don't leave," the chief ordered, then he was gone.

Qemal hung up the receiver, went out of the booth, and sat on a bench at the end of the empty hall. He felt ill at ease. The order of the branch chief was strange, incomprehensible. Qemal felt in some way as though taken into custody. Why the heck did I do this, he asked himself, now I'm in a mess. But why would they arrest me? On what charge? No, this is impossible, this can't be, no way! The chief ordered him to wait there because apparently he would come in person to discuss the case, which was quite intricate and could not be explained correctly over the phone. Yes, yes. The chief's order is no surprise, my supposition of feeling detained is. True, I do not dare budge from here, but what's the connection between detention and my actions! Because I did what had to be done, nothing else. Exactly. Actually it is all about an extremely complicated case. And an extremely important one. That worry in the chief's voice, that anxiety even. Or was Qemal himself experiencing the anxiety and trying to shift its burden onto something else outside himself? They'll either promote me or demobilize me, he thought, torn by indecision. This is a big question mark. If things go well, everything will go well for me too, because I was the first to find out. But, if it turns out to be a goose egg, I'm done for. The anxiety overwhelming him was becoming more and more unbearable. His mind was going haywire. For brief moments he managed to persuade himself that most signs indicated for the better outcome and he found some solace in that, and then quite suddenly this belief made his wait more agonizing. So much so that he felt he would rather brood over the opposite, that all of this was only a goose egg, a flash in the pan, and he would be demobilized and would have to work as an ordinary laborer in a factory or in construction or in cargo handling or worse, and more believably, he would be deported for reeducation to some village, to toil and moil from dawn till dusk, and remain forever a lone wolf, forlorn and forsaken until his dog days, like those miserable old duffers who roam the streets all day long not knowing what to do or what the point of living is. At this, anguish almost stifled him and again he strove to persuade himself of the opposite, that is, of his promotion. And those opposite conclusions were each equally probable and improbable. Only a fortune-teller could find out, he thought by and by. Can fortune-tellers see the future of things, is it possible to precede time? This time thing is so incomprehensible, a tangle the human mind is unable to unravel.

This reminded him of his grandmother again. Once, many many years ago, in his early childhood, his grandmother had told him a story about some gargantuan serpent, or dragon, or Hydra that devoured time interminably, and so time was spent and consumed because what this Hydra swallowed could not come back. But now anything might happen. Just as that man had come back from the world of the dead, from whence there is no return, the Hydra that gulps down time might throw it up again, thus reversing time, so that what has not yet happened would happen before what has already happened. He was at the point of persuading himself that fortune-telling might be true. But the branch chief had ordered him to wait there at the post office and not go anywhere. In fact it took about one hour and twenty minutes from the district branch building to here, but the order was for him to wait, even for the rest of his life, and an order is an order. Right. But Qemal, impatient and overwhelmingly anxious to learn what the future had in store for him, would not mind playing some teeny-weeny trick on this order, so that in the time interval before the arrival of those from the branch he could go out and look for that woman who had talked on the phone and through her find that very skillful fortune-teller and ask her to read his fortune. He thought that he should at least go out and look around, do something for God's sake. Thoughts still awash with these reflections, he was about to get up and go when, through the glass in the hallway, he saw the stout woman walking across the street. He dashed out and headed in her direction, though not quite sure by now whether it was the same woman. He ventured to speak to her.

"Please, Comrade . . . "

"Yes, Comrade," she said as if annoyed.

"Can you please tell me where that fortune-teller lives, that famous fortune-teller . . . "

"I'm not a fortune-teller! I don't know anything about them, leave me alone . . . "

She didn't understand. It wasn't her, Qemal thought, but then he insisted.

"Listen," he said sternly. "And don't yell at me! I am a Sigurimi officer and you have to respond promptly."

"My, my," the woman muttered, and her face turned ashen. "Be a darling. Don't drive me to ruin and leave my children uncared for."

She is probably not the woman at the telephone booth but this one knows where I can find the fortune-teller, Qemal thought.

"Listen," he said, toning down. "I did not say that you are a fortune-teller and I have nothing against you. What I want from you is to tell me where the fortune-teller lives . . . the best in the city . . . "

"Be a darling, don't ruin me," the woman said. "I can take you there."

Off they went, she in the lead and he following two or three steps behind.

They crossed a bridge and came to an old neighborhood with sprawling low houses on the other side of the river. In one of the narrow alleys, not far from the riverbank, the woman stopped and pointed to a door, but she did not dare come any closer.

"Okay, be gone now!" Qemal said. "And you'll be sorry if you lied to me."

Qemal knocked on the door. After some time a woman dressed in black opened the door. He gave the name of the fortune-teller just as the guide had advised him to do. The woman in black frowned ·in disbelief for a split second, glanced down both sides of the alley, then whispered provocatively, "It is me. Today is not a good day for fortune-telling. You should have come yesterday. Yesterday was a Friday . . . "

"Uh, have a nice day," Qemal said.

He turned to go and she spoke again, lips curling in an almost invisible smile, "You may come next Friday . . . reading cards two hundred leks, coffee cup reading three hundred . . . "

"I'll come," Qemal said. "Sure I will."

Just like a whore, he said to himself upon leaving. Qemal had imagined that the fortune-teller would be a scrawny, cadaverous old hag, while this one was much younger and nearly presentable. He'd like to come again on Friday, not for the fortune-telling, because that wouldn't be necessary by that time, but to tell her who he really was, tell her where he worked, and then after intimidating her, he would start a conversation in the way that only he could, by probing her with his only eye, then taking the money from his pocket and putting it in front of her, and she, startled and relieved, would think the money was for fortune-telling, but he would bring it out to ask for something else and she'd have to consent, money or no money now, she would acquiesce out of fear but he would pay her nonetheless, and in return, he'd tell her she was a whore and he would tell her again before she surrendered to him as a whore and repeat it once more before she gave herself to him, and during intercourse he would whisper obscene words to her. And he would do it without taking off all her black clothes. And for this there was no need to wait until Friday, which was a good day for fortune-telling. He looked behind him to fix the gate in his memory, the fence painted in white, the luxurious tree branches entwined over the fence. But wait, there was something else awaiting him. He did not know how the case of the dead man would end. Whether he would continue to be in the Sigurimi or whether he would be discharged. Where he would be on Friday, or even today in an hour or so. He had to wait, he had no choice. It was the first time in his life that he had felt helpless, unable to cope with what was in store for him and what might very well be his demise. If only he could disappear. Disappear just like that Viktor who had perished in the sea. To lose himself, to become one with the river waters or the mist lingering over the hills, over the river banks, and over the forest. But he did not know how to do this, so could do nothing but wait and obey orders, as always, submissively. He had to go back to where he was ordered to wait. There was some time left before their arrival and in the meantime he could drink another glass.

■ □ ■ □ ■

CHAPTER THREE

The earth opened up slowly.

THE MINISTER HUNG UP THE HOTLINE RECEIVER THAT CONNECTED him instantly to the Leader. As was often the case lately, he was overwhelmed by a vague feeling of uneasiness tinged with adoration and superstitious fear. So he would meet with the Leader twice that day, which was unprecedented; this was the day of days in this interminable time since the Leader had lost his sight completely. This evening he would go with other Politburo members to wish him a happy birthday, but in just two hours he and the Leader would have a tête-à-tête. Some Politburo members had not met with the Leader for years, except for the rare occasions when he appeared in front of the people, while he, the Minister of the Interior, his secret forechosen successor, was going to meet with him twice that day. And since the Leader had summoned him to such an unusual meeting, that meant that the Leader had assessed the tidings he sent him and was waiting to hear some other important issues, and he, the Minister of the Interior, would in turn hear some important ideas from the Leader that could not otherwise be conveyed over the hotline. The minister threw an apologetic glance at the phone as if to curry favor with this unknown black animal that had come from God knows what planet, and that was gradually calming down and dozing off, turning into a lifeless, petrified, impenetrable idol, an ominous sphinx, a totem. Carefully, not to awaken it, his stare glided over the piece of paper on the table, a report that had just arrived from the chief of the N—— District Branch. Between the lines and on the margins the paper was full of remarks in red, most of them senseless, scribbled simply in fury. It was very difficult to make out from this blurred report something definite that could be related to the Leader. It was as if the person who wrote it had scrawled on it mercilessly, smearing it with blood. No, it was the letter itself that portended blood, the idea flashing across the minister's mind. And almost simultaneously he recalled something that his rival, Ferhat, had said when they were hunting last Sunday for the first time after so many years. We miss drenching our mustaches in blood, as we did in our youth, Ferhat told him, exhilarated by the restored friendship, nostalgic from reminiscing, transfigured by sleeplessness that late night, after having finished the last card game. We'll dip them in your blood, said the minister to himself. He was filled with a sudden gust of exuberance. He jumped to his feet and started pacing to and fro in his office, mulling the Leader's phone call over repeatedly, attending to every nuance, making sure that he had grasped the Leader's understatement correctly, that he had not faltered, that there was indeed something extremely priceless in this, something that he as Minister of the Interior could in no way let slip through his fingers. The arrival of a subversive agent after a quarter century, during which time nobody dared set foot on this soil, is another proof of the Leader's brilliant thesis that during all that time foreign enemies did not forget us, as some ninnies would have us think. On the contrary, foreign enemies have always had us in the bull's-eye, working relentlessly to undermine and overthrow our people's power, and what is more, all the internal enemy groups destroyed time after time were tools in their hands. There's even more to it. For some time now there have been no internal enemy groups, or to be more precise none have been eliminated, for it is impossible that such groups do not exist. The Leader's statement implied that the sudden arrival, or seemingly sudden arrival, of the subversive agent shows on the other hand that we have to be vigilant and keep our eyes open. This recollection of the Leader's statement sent shivers down the minister's spine. When he had first heard it he was unable to grasp its full meaning, as he was always overwhelmed when he spoke over the hotline, or probably because the Leader had mentioned eyes, which always spurred certain feelings of guilt in the minister. Unquestionably the words he recalled were those of the Leader. He had not added something to them himself as he did unconsciously whenever he conversed with him about such issues, the more so as he found it more and more difficult to separate the Leader's statements from his own conjectures, which had never let him down, because he was more and more becoming one with the Leader. But sometimes it was necessary to separate the statements from the conjectures because the Leader and he were not one and the same, there was only one Leader. But for this statement he was absolutely sure. And its meaning, which he could only dimly guess at a moment ago, was crystal clear in his mind, and it could not be otherwise. We miss drenching our mustaches in blood. Now I have you in my grip, thought the minister, still pacing his office, as his shadow under the yellowish light of the lampshade on the writing table glided over the walls, an impenetrable, omnipotent jinni of the fairy tales, sometimes getting smaller but more pronounced and sometimes getting bigger and more blurred. Now I have you in my grip. Much more so because from the start of the conversation, the Leader had made mention of something that had to do with internal and external enemies. So. The other issue pertaining to the order to keep the subversive agent under constant surveillance while allowing him to proceed on his journey could have no meaning other than that the Leader was convinced the subversive agent had come to meet with someone who was not just a random person. And this someone is you, Ferhat, the minister growled to himself. It's you, Ferhat, nobody else. We miss drenching our mustaches in blood as we once did in our youth. The weekend they went hunting together, the minister was also overwhelmed by the memories of their old friendship. But then, the next day, as soon as he woke up, his hatred for Ferhat, the acrimony that had started God knows how and that rendered their confrontation inevitable, came back. The Minister of the Interior could not prevaricate as did Ferhat, his rival who was doomed because of it. Or better, he was doomed, therefore he prevaricated in an effort to soothe his mind. Because deep down he was afraid of the minister. Deep down he had a premonition that the minister would blow his head off, not the other way around. Though Ferhat was still more powerful than the minister, this was only in appearance. Therefore that unexpected invitation to go hunting together seemed to come from a very distant time, from once upon a time. To perjure yourself, he addressed Ferhat in his mind. There is nothing else you could do. To stay put awaiting your doomsday for days, weeks, months, completely helpless to defy it, this must be unbearable. Shouldn't it be? Subsequently better perjure yourself. That's it. However, not apprehending the unknown newcomer promptly was not to the minister's liking. This was meddling with his calculations even. Because what if, in pursuit of his mission, the unknown newcomer who had arrived from beyond the sun, that is, the subversive agent, went somewhere he shouldn't and met someone unintentionally, that is, not exactly unintentionally because he has an objective, but suppose he goes and meets with someone and entangles matters to such an extent that it becomes impossible to find a lead to connect him with others we are aiming at, or to be more precise, with a single one, the big spider in its dark corner, spinning the web of conspiracy that we must foil. Spiders. This is how Ferhat had branded the conspirators many years ago when the first conspiracy was disclosed and thwarted. The Leader himself had borrowed the word from Ferhat and had made it his own, regurgitating it again and again like an incantation. The spiders multiplied and thrived everywhere, in his speeches, in Politburo meetings, in plenary sessions of the Party Central Committee, in conferences, and in the media, intermingled with other pungent words that seemed to tear and rip them apart. Spiders, spiders, spiders. Spiders here and there and everywhere. And the Interior Minister, resorting to guesswork, sniffed them out, ferreted them out from their murky hiding places, where they crouched to weave their sinister conspiracy webs, and brought them into broad daylight, infallibly so, because the Leader guided the path, especially when the spider happened to be massive and covered under seven shadowy layers in such a manner that only the Leader could discern its presence. And only by resorting to guesswork was it possible to dig them out of their murky immobility and camouflage. This time, however, it was different. This time the Leader lay in wait, he wanted to see the conspirators make the first move and uncover themselves no matter how little. What is it? the minister asked himself. Is the Leader convinced that we are dealing with a conspiracy, with a true conspiracy, that is? All conspiracies have been true, he responded with an internal scream, finding himself in the grip of a terrible suspicion, which made him shudder with distant fear, similar to the horror he once felt, as a small child, in the presence of spiders. No, the Leader has always been right, he has always been hawk-eyed and farsighted, he has always foiled the conspirators without any leads, and it has always come to what the Leader foresaw, said the minister to himself, as if in a fervent prayer that tried to chase away a malevolent temptation. And as for me, his Interior Minister, I have served him zealously and dutifully by untangling the conspiracy webs and bringing the spiders out of their dark spots, with the Leader's sharp eye lighting the way because he can see things others cannot, as for example now, in spite of his slightly different behavior. The Leader knows what he is doing, he knows these things better, and it will come out for the better. The minister would have continued this stream of supplicatory monologue if it were not for the telephone ring that cut him short, it was the special ring used only by the hotline.

"Hello, at your service," said the minister after picking up the receiver hurriedly.

It was the Leader himself. With his deep voice and slow speech, stammering a little with age, he asked the Interior Minister whether he had good records of the burial of the remains of that poet, musician, what's his name, oh, yes, Viktor Dragoti.

"Yes, there are, sir," the minister answered in one breath. "There must be for sure . . . Before I come to you I'll go to the archives and look for them myself . . . "

No, no he should not take the trouble, the Leader was satisfied with the answer. Then he said something about having the subversive agent under continuous surveillance and then hung up. The minister held the receiver to his ear for another minute or so and then put it down. Then his gaze carefully stole away from the black thing, still alive, still ready to scream its shivering scream, and stopped short for a moment on the bloody paper that was still squirming on the table, and then rested on the electronic clock next to the lamp. It was not yet two. I have plenty of time, he thought, to dart off to the archives. He stood up and strolled out of his office. The burial of Viktor's remains must be in the records but he would go to the archives to see for himself, urged by an obscure craving for the impossible. Because he wished this stranger, whose every step toward Tirana was kept under surveillance, to be Viktor Dragoti. Because at the time when Viktor Dragoti, the poet and musician, was killed by the border guard, more precisely the coast guard, as he tried to escape by swimming to ships anchored offshore, outside the harbor, seemingly the Leader remembered something about this case; at that time, nine years ago, the coast guard was still under the Ministry of Defense and Ferhat was then the minister of defense; consequently, if the subversive agent was Viktor Dragoti, it could come out very clearly that he was not killed nine years ago, and that it was only a game played by Ferhat so that he could send Viktor to the other side, to his foreign intelligence masters who would send him back again eventually, when they determined that the time was right, while on the other hand, to accomplish all of this, Ferhat fabricated a nonexistent murder. But Viktor Dragoti was killed and the subversive agent could not be him, though the operative who first encountered the stranger, and who was now locked up in a madhouse, swore to the contrary till he was blue in the face. The Interior Minister knew it could not happen, he had seen the cadaver with his own eyes, it was washed ashore by the waves after about a week, fish bites all over, and his forensic experts confirmed the identification of the body. Oh, well, actually that is not important. Most important, the Leader himself assumed that Ferhat might be the one to have employed subterfuge, or even if the Leader did not make any assumptions but thought of it, knowing it was not true, in any case the Leader was after Ferhat this time and he had implied this to the minister most suggestively. I'm such a fool not to have grasped it, the minister chuckled. After all, this is what happens when Lady Luck knocks on your door. This was really great, a fortunate outcome that came as a reward with very little toil on his part. He had always sensed that he would be his rival's downfall, but that it would be so easy, that he would do it with such incredible effortlessness, he could never have imagined. But so it was, whether he liked it or not, and he wanted it by all means, and since he wanted it, just a little effort on his part, a very little effort, and everything would go as he wished. His temples started thump thumping, his heart swelled, and the minister could hardly breathe for exultation. To take his mind off that and calm down, he went to the window and started to look out between the slats of the venetian blinds, which had not been replaced since before the War when the edifice was erected. Passersby loomed ahead on the sidewalk that ran along the Ministry of the Interior, with some kind of indifference, as if the building were just like any other building. With contrived indifference or innocence, the minister thought, because in our midst are enemies, all equally innocent in appearance. As usual, he rejoiced over this view as he watched them from above, small, suppressed, obscure insects crawling sluggishly. By now he had cooled off a bit. And he cheered up. Before going to the archives he thought to give his mistress Magda a call. He returned to his desk and sat down. Then, instinctively shunning the black phone, he reached for the white one with a cheerful gleam and started dialing the number. But before he could get through, he realized in bewilderment that he was not dialing his mistress's number but Ferhat's, his rival's. And yet he dialed the number in full. What am I doing, he wondered. From the day they went hunting, they had neither seen nor called each other. He was pretty certain, however, that Ferhat was the same inveterate nostalgic person of that weekend. Nostalgic out of necessity, the minister thought between two dial tones ringing on the other end, he has been waiting for my call all this time, waiting in anguish, like a deflowered girl waiting on her lover's subsequent behavior. That instant he heard Ferhat's voice.

"Hello . . . yes, it's me," the minister said, doing his best to add a merry timbre to his voice.

"I haven't heard from you in a long time," Ferhat said, his voice wavering.

Son of a bitch, snapped the minister, motherfucker. Then he added aloud, "I've been up to my neck in work, and I've been thinking of calling you . . . How are you? . . . I was worried when you didn't call."

"I've been doing well," Ferhat replied, "But we'll see each other today, won't we, at the Leader's office. It'll be a great pleasure to meet with the Leader, after such a long time . . ."

The tongue ever turns to the aching tooth. But now I'll curdle your blood, the Interior Minister swore under his breath.

"Yes, sure. And I'll even have a tête-à-tête with him before that."

"Oh," Ferhat's voice sank, though he managed to utter, "that is a greater pleasure . . . it is luck . . ."

"That's right." The Interior Minister felt repugnance mounting and was about to discontinue the conversation, but making another painful effort added, "You know why I called you? When are we going hunting again?"

That was something, he told himself.

"We can go tonight," Ferhat shrieked.

"No, not tonight, we can't," he replied. "Tomorrow we have to attend other activities in honor of the Leader . . . "

"Oh, yes, it slipped my mind!"

"What about next weekend?" the Interior Minister said.

"Sure! We can leave on Saturday afternoon and Sunday morning we go hunting. Okay?"

"Okay. So, till next Saturday."

May you not see it in freedom, he said, again in an undertone, as he put the receiver down. That invitation to go hunting was something. The Interior Minister was satisfied with himself. And he was rejoicing. Let's call Magda. He dialed her number, his face beaming with a broad, lusty smile, as if he had her right there in front of him. Again it was her father that picked up the phone.

"Hello, can I talk to Magda please?"

"Yes, hold on please . . . "

Since her divorce she lived alone with her father. He recognizes your voice, Magda told him once. Does your father know who I am, the minister inquired of his mistress. No, no way. No other male calls me, which is why he doesn't ask. Nevertheless, the minister had some people follow her every move, spying on whom she met with, until he was convinced she wasn't cheating.

"Hi, sweetheart, is that you?"

"Yes, my dear, it's me. What are you doing?"

"Oh, I was lying down, resting," Magda drawled her vowels co-quettishly. "This morning we had a rehearsal again."

The minister began to salivate.

"Can we meet tonight, my darling?" he asked.

"Tonight is the show," Magda replied, with the same coquetry, uttering the words virtually in a sigh.

"When does the show end?" the minister asked.

"By about 6:30 or 7:00 P.M.," the sigh rang in his ears.

"Very well, until then I'll be busy too," the minister said. "We'll meet with the Leader. Can we meet after the show? What do you think?"

Not like this, he added to himself, realizing that he was almost pleading, recognizing as always a certain power she had over him, a certain unavoidable power, a certain right to oppose him, as he waited anxiously for her reply.

"Yes," she said at last in a faint voice. "You can come."

"Then at about 7:00 P.M. I'll be there, at the rendezvous," the minister said, trying to hide his anguish.

"I'll be waiting for you. See you then, dear . . . "

She could not say otherwise, thought the minister, putting down the receiver, and all of a sudden he felt he had become ridiculous by entreating her a minute ago as if he were a greenhorn and not the Interior Minister, one of the most powerful people in the country, the most powerful after the Leader, and tomorrow the Leader himself. After pressing a button at his table to say he wanted his car ready, he went out of the office and descended the stairs, as the pleasure of his power over his secret mistress mingled with skeptical misgiving lest she loathed him deep down, a suspicion that made his desire to hold sway over her more nagging.

His car was waiting at the main gate, the one on Martyrs of the Nation Boulevard. There on the sidewalk in front of the building stood some transfixed passersby and a series of recently pruned trees, resembling guards with their overhanging, lifeless trunks and shrunken male limbs. As he got into the backseat of the car, he told the chauffeur to drive in the direction of the archives. The archives were located on the outskirts of the city. Leaving behind the last quarter of the eastern suburbs and the rumbling noise that came from a huge industrial construction site that grew from year to year and yet retained the shapeless form of something that had just begun to be built, the car continued along the winding roads through the rambling hills between the city and the foot of Dajti Mountain. Patches of mist were still hanging over the hills. The archives were undetectable from the paved roadway, the slope of a hill obstructed the view. Thank God there is no rain, the minister thought, as the car made a turn onto a narrow alley with asphalt eroded by rain, because he could not go to the Leader in a car smeared in mud. After going uphill and then downhill two or three times, the car drove up a low-lying hill smaller than the surrounding ones, with a two-story building perched on its top. A lonely quadrangle building. The minister would have taken it for a water depot had he not known that this was the building of the Interior Ministry Archives. Recognizing his car from afar, the director appeared at the gate to welcome him.

"I wish you good health, Comrade Minister."

"Good health to you. Well, how are things going?" the minister asked almost mechanically.

"Well, Comrade Minister," the archive director responded promptly.

The director led the minister to the upper floor where he had transferred his office since accepting the position of acting Special Fund chief, because the former chief had suffered a nervous breakdown and, given that the position was very important, they thought it would be better if the director himself assumed the responsibility. They crossed the antechamber of the Special Fund, where a team of experts from the ministry were working, and proceeded to his office.

"I haven't much to do here," the minister said as he took the archive director's seat and the director himself sat on another chair opposite him. "I have just come to look at the burial process file of someone killed in a defection attempt. He was killed, if I am not mistaken, in 1967 . . . Yes, exactly."

"We keep such records here, in the Special Fund," the archive director said. "I'll go and fetch it."

"Hurry, I need it as soon as possible . . . "

The director dashed out of the room and the minister remained alone in the office. He waited in his seat for a moment and then impatiently rose and started to pace the room. Moments seemed interminably long. Not that they seemed long. The director was taking longer than expected. After some time the minister opened the door and came to the antechamber where the team of experts were working. They took their eyes off the files, as if in confusion, then one after the other stood up.

"Sit down, sit down, go on with your work," the minister said.

They bent again over the stacks piled in front of them, occasionally picking one or several pages or an entire bundle of documents from a file and then bringing them together to form another bundle, another file, thus begetting little by little, some new files. Looking at them, it dawned quite suddenly on the minister that there was some similarity between their work and the occasional exhumation of the executed who were later buried somewhere else. The archive director came in. The minister's eye caught his ashen face and then his empty hands. The director was looking at him in bewilderment and did not speak.

"Come on," the minister said, making for the office, he did not want to talk in front of the others.

"They could not find it, Comrade Minister," the director said, closing the door behind him and trembling.

"Hmm, couldn't you find out whether one of our experts has it, I mean . . . " the minister tried to contain his jubilation and at the same time make sure matters stood just as he wanted them.

"No," the director said with his eyes wide open with trepidation. "None of them has it and there is not even a card index."

"Don't worry." The minister felt pity for the man and tried to soothe him. "Perhaps there was not a file on that person."

"Oh, no, Comrade Minister," the archive director stammered. "We had such a file. I'm sure of this, Comrade Minister. I saw that file two or three days ago with my own eyes, I swear on my eyes," and he branched his fingers in front of his eyes as if poking into them.

"Come," the minister said, bringing a smile to his face. "Don't do that. Resume your work, no need to worry. We will take care of the rest."

"At your orders, Comrade Minister."

"That's good, and don't tremble like a leaf in the wind. Well, good-bye . . . "

In the meantime the minister was also trembling; he was experiencing a pleasurable shiver that went down his spine, what he learned was so unanticipated and so desirable.

So, the file is missing, he pondered, jolting in his car as the chauffeur took quick turns, shooting back toward the city. The file was there before but now it isn't. Somebody gained access to the archives and removed the file. Somebody who is one step down in the hierarchy, who was caught in the intricate black conspiracy web. Or somebody else who has authority over those below me, and who for this reason is a little above me, such as Ferhat, for example. Another thread leads to Ferhat. Well, what about the thread that extended to his own ministry, where does that lead? Which one of his subordinates might have some special connection with his rival? And apparently old ties? Because how could the file disappear otherwise? As the car wound through the sparse but chaotic traffic of buses and trucks going back and forth in the industrial zone, he thought it would probably be worthwhile to go see that person in charge of the Archive

Special Fund who went insane a few days before. He looked at his watch. He had enough time to pay a short visit to the psychiatric hospital on his way back. First talk to Basri, who was his confidante. He told the chauffeur to drive him there. Then he lowered the dark curtains of the back windows on both sides so that no one could see him entering the psychiatric hospital. All the cars of the Politburo members have the same curtains, he thought, let them think of whomever they like. And the license plates could be changed. He would tell the chauffeur to change them today.

As the car turned in the direction of the hospital courtyard, he sank into the backseat to hide himself from the curious eyes of some individuals waiting on the sidewalk. The car made slowly for the courtyard and stopped in front of the patio. The minister told his bodyguard to find the psychiatric ward chief and bring him out to the car. There were some patients strolling randomly in the courtyard, some in a hurry, some at leisure, others were standing petrified in various poses. One of them approached the car, bent over its windshield, and started to open and close his mouth as if biting into something. Look how low man can fall, thought the minister. The chauffeur was gesturing to the patient to move away from the car.

"Easy, easy, he's not going to eat you," the minister said.

"I don't want him to soil it," the chauffeur said.

"At least he'd clean it," said the minister. "It was already soiled when we went to the archives."

"No," the chauffeur said, "Only the tires got muddy and a little splash here and there . . . Even the tires got cleaned on our way here."

The minister looked at his watch. Good, he said to himself, otherwise there wouldn't be enough time to have the car washed before I go to see the Leader. As Doctor Basri was descending the stairs followed by the minister's bodyguard, the patient looking through the windshield bowed in a sign of respect and left hastily, looking frightened and guilty. They too know what fear is, said the minister to himself, while the doctor sat on the passenger seat by his side.

"Is there anything new?" the minister asked, as they shook hands.

"About an hour ago they brought in the operative from the N——District Branch," Basri said, "and according to your orders I shut him in an isolation room."

"How is he?"

"From the examination he appears completely normal," Basri whispered. "He was a little drunk but became sober very quickly. Now, hardly an hour in the isolation room and he is in a depressive mood, probably the consequence of claustrophobia . . . "

"Which means . . . "

"He cannot put up with isolation. But claustrophobia affects people in different ways."

This is what happens to people in detention, thought the minister. The worse for Qemal because he finds himself in the same quandary as those whom he has apprehended and on whom he exercised his power. That is the reason he's gone completely insane.

"What is he doing, how does he show his lunacy?" the minister asked.

"He wrangles with himself, shrieks, squeals, whines. And he is in delirium and raving all the time, occasionally repeating dialogue from the movie *The Adventures of Ulysses* that has been playing in theaters recently."

"Hmm," the minister grimaced. "Interesting . . . what about the other one, Naun Gjika, how is he?"

"Poles apart," the doctor said. "He's really ailing."

"What is he doing?"

"His behavior is bizarre. From the very start he asked for pen and paper. We provided him with pen and paper to see what he was going to do. He divided the paper into smaller pieces, wrote on them and then burned them. We removed his matches so that we could see what he was writing, but as soon as he'd hear the door open he would put the pieces of paper into his mouth, chew, and swallow them instantly . . . "

"You couldn't get anything?" the minister asked, his curiosity aroused.

"Not a single one," said the doctor. "We then put an informer in his room but Naun stopped writing altogether. Now he is alone again but he is not writing any more. He does not speak. He does not reply to anything, as if he were deaf and dumb. Or pretending to be."

"This case of burned or disposed pieces of paper is interesting," the minister fretted. "Can we go and see them?"

"Sure," Basri said, turning to open the car door.

"No, wait," the minister said. "I don't want anyone to see me here . . . Rumors might flare up about me, you get it?" he added as if joking.

"No problem," the doctor said, "The isolation rooms are in a separate section of the building. We can go there from the back. There is no one there."

The minister ordered the chauffeur to start the car, and as Basri showed the way, they circled the building and drove into a tiny deserted backyard.

"Let's enter here," the doctor said, pointing at a secluded side door.

As they got out of the car, the doctor opened a small door and led the minister through a narrow corridor, poorly lit by dim light coming from the windows. The doctor halted in front of one of the heavy bolted doors lining the entire length of the corridor and quietly opened a nearly invisible slit. The minister looked through it. For an instant he was blinded by the whiteness of the isolation room. Everything was white, indistinguishable for a fraction of a second, but for the man who was floating in the air over his white bed, motionless, with a fixed gaze somewhere in the empty space in front of him.

"This is how he sits all day long because he thinks he's being surveyed."

"Can you bring him out of this state?" the minister asked. "I mean when can you make him speak up?"

The doctor shrugged his shoulders.

"Where is the other one?" the minister inquired.

Basri went to the other door and opened the slit. Through it the minister could see a strangely contorted creature pacing the room with his hands on his head, rumpling his hair and clawing his cheeks, moaning and complaining at the same time. The minister could not hear him from the outside so he put his ear to the slit to hear better.

"Ooh, you Nobody, what have you done to me," he could hear the voice of the isolated man say through moans . . . "Nobody blinded me . . . made me drunk with wine and then plucked out my only eye. Help, help brothers . . . It was Nobody . . . Nobody . . . ooh . . ."

The minister moved his head away from the slit and shut it.

"What if you put these two together?" he asked the doctor, uncertain as to why he said it.

"We can try," the doctor said.

"And if anything new comes out, please call me immediately . . . "

Then the minister dashed out. He had barely jumped into the car when the chauffeur accelerated in the direction of the Bllok.* Two or three times he goaded the chauffeur to drive faster, but it was difficult for the driver to do that while avoiding the pedestrians who became more numerous as they approached the center. As they reached a busy and chaotic intersection, bang, the car swung into an old woman crossing the street, knocking her right onto the asphalt. Honking, screeching brakes.

Bang.

"Oh, my God," the chauffeur said.

"Drive on," the minister pressed him.

The car plowed straight ahead, at a higher speed, avoiding the eyes of the pedestrians, their stunned faces, all with the same blank and rigid expression. Rigidity that had some meaning. It implied something. Rigidity as a sign of respect for our power, thought the minister, overwhelmed. Rigidityrespect. Of course, they were expecting me to get her to the hospital, that is why their faces looked so bewildered. That is why they were frozen into masks. Confusion, shock for what happened but also because of something else. Confusion, shock because they do not know how to explain it. They do not dare say we are worse than the bourgeoisie and landlords, against whom we rose and fought and overthrew, hence that shock, that myriad of expressionless faces turned to masks. Because they do not know how to express what is intended to be expressed without their knowledge and against their will. Because they do not want to express it willingly. Because they know something else, which is that only the enemy says that we are worse than the bourgeoisie and the landlords we overthrew. The enemies yes, they can say that. It is better for us that the enemies say it because in this way others are deterred from following suit. For that reason they shun one another, they even guard themselves from evil thinking, and what remains is only emptiness because they have nothing to think about, the minister churned in

*The guarded residential area for Politburo members.

his mind. Because they find it difficult to comprehend we have no time to go back, we have other things to do, we have to press on because we have work to do for their well-being, rescuing them from a far worse evil than that which befell that poor woman, an evil menacing everybody, all the people, that is. However, the minister thought, loosening his tie, what happened and how it happened, the manner in which I left the scene, could never be imagined when we rose to fight against them. Even less when we overthrew them. As they drove by all eyes turned to the car. By now the minister guessed all had already learned about the incident. At last they crossed the Blood of Martyrs Square and the car headed hastily through Martyrs of the Nation Boulevard to the Bllok. He was on time, even a little early. For the well-being of the people, the minister repeated to himself, always for the well-being of the people. To avoid any malevolence befalling the people. To rescue them from an abysmal evil nestled at the pinnacle of leadership. As the car took the last slow turn in one of the inner streets of the Bllok, he was reminded of some piece of intelligence about what they below, the people, said whenever somebody from the leadership was branded an enemy. The people's abhorrence poured over that enemy to such extent that the minister suspected it was an older, suppressed aversion that in this way found release. He thought that deep down this suspicion had gnawed at him from the beginning. From the very beginning. Would people act toward me in the same way, would they reminisce about what happened today to the old woman? The frozen masks thawed, the beastly face of the lunatic appeared in the background of multiplied mouths opened not to speak but to bite. To shred me to pieces. They would be right were it not that he had to perform the task he had undertaken, the task that was the reason he had left in such haste. He tried to calm down. We have so much work to do, he thought, so much work and this is what detaches us from the people. It seems to detach us from the people, that is. Therefore everything depends on the honesty with which we perform that with which we are entrusted, this is the proof in the pudding of the loyalty and determination to the cause of the people in the uncompromising struggle against their enemies. To cave in the enemies, to wipe them out. He tightened the knot of his tie and looked at his watch. He had a few more minutes to wait there, in that flat pancake square, girdled by the mansions of the Bllok, in a kind of a garden with artificial bushes, sparsely dotted with trees, the location of a nonexistent or vanished mansion. In the meantime, everything he experienced earlier with the old woman in a far-off intersection became alien, unreal, eerie. He squinted at his watch again, then got out of the automobile under the electronic scrutiny of a series of cameras hidden nearby. He had just enough time to sort out in his mind what he had to report to the Leader, because at that moment somewhere in the square, the ground shifted and a gaping entry opened slowly to an underground passage, the secret quarters of the Leader, and the minister started to descend.

■ □ ■ □ ■

CHAPTER FOUR

May favorable winds steer you wherever you go . . .

IT WAS STILL DAYLIGHT AS VIKTOR DRAGOTI HEADED TOWARD
downtown after getting off the bus that had brought him to the capi-
tal, but though he did not have far to go and walked briskly, when he
arrived at Blood of Martyrs Square dusk had already set in. The
square was almost as deserted as the streets, with only a few pedestrians hurrying along. Wind was blowing and it seemed the rain would
pour down at any minute, but for now it was drizzling, with the raindrops being carried away by the wind. At last the neon lights came on
and for a moment everything seemed frozen under their whitening
glow. Viktor felt estranged, in a strange city, amid an asphalt space
that looked more desolate because he knew that trees had once grown
there; the linden trees and wild chestnut trees had disappeared. New
cumbersome buildings lumbered on ahead, with stark white facades,
no glass spaces, blinding in their uniformity and whiteness, with
rows upon rows of limestone or marble columns rising instead of
trees. He was in a dreamlike state. Am I here or not, is it Tirana or
not, he kept repeating to himself. Yet there was something sinister in
this marbled whiteness and glimmer, as if the buildings were the offspring of a dangerously tricky subterfuge and an icy seraglio where a
witch had her home. He had such a thirst for life, yet it was mixed
with a feeling of estrangement because the attractions of this life demanded adaptation, demanded submissiveness in return. He felt that
the ugly, gloomy buildings that were there when he left had seemed
to him more acceptable and more intimate. All things considered, he

thought there was some truth in their ugliness. However, Viktor felt somehow fascinated and allured by this world. At least it aroused his inquisitiveness. He stopped in front of movie posters. The two main movie theaters, named 8 November in commemoration of the Party's birthday and 16 October in honor of the Leader's birthday, were showing *The Adventures of Ulysses*. The title was written in bright colors and the letters resembled bits and pieces of marble fortresses in flames. Viktor remembered having seen this movie on a foreign TV station years ago. He drew closer to get a better view of the pictures. Nausicaa. There is Polyphemus in his cave, blinded. Opposite a picture of cannibals. Proteus. Circe. Ulysses in the underworld with the dead. In a close-up, the ominous rocks of the Sirens and the hardly visible boat, cornered somewhere in the background. The god of winds, then Eumaeus. Polyphemus outside the cave, bawling. There is Penelope. And again Polyphemus. Viktor's gaze paused unexpectedly at a picture bigger than the rest of a half-naked woman in a seductive pose, it was the singer who played Circe, he could not recall her name. Then he got the feeling that he should leave. It was not because of the freezing raindrops occasionally falling on his hair and face nor the chilliness that made him turn up the collar of his jacket, shrug his shoulders, and pull in his neck. It was something else, a hazy awareness, indistinguishable at first, but soon crystal clear, of being observed. There was nobody to be seen but he still had the feeling he was under constant and persistent surveillance. He quickened his steps through the square with no specific direction in mind, simply to avoid the scrutinizing eye. But that eye was zooming in. He hesitated to turn his head. Meanwhile he noticed he was in front of the Palace of Concerts, a huge white edifice he had not recognized a little earlier since its facade had changed: now it had a marble facing and had almost doubled in size. However, he thought, I know all its ins and outs. So better go inside to avoid my pursuer. As he approached the corner of the building with the intention of sweeping around and entering through one of the numerous back doors, he quickened his steps and heard the echo of footsteps chasing him. Viktor rushed more hastily and the footsteps rushed after him. He had hardly reached the corner when he broke into a run, dashed through an open door at the back of the building, and on up a flight of stairs, climbing two and three steps at a time. As he paused on the landing between the second and the third flights of stairs to catch his breath, he heard rushing footsteps from down below. With almost maniacal vigor Viktor ran toward the upper level, climbing and climbing, in search of a door, but none were to be found, while the footsteps came closer and closer, or at least this is what he imagined, and glancing back he saw the pursuer right below, he could see one leg and one arm and half a body ascending in haste, come on, I have to run faster or else he'll catch up, but where could he go farther, a little farther up and he'd land on the top floor, and there at the end of the stairs he saw a door, and immediately recalled it was the door to the vestiary, at all times under lock and key, yet he made for it and fortunately enough it was unlocked, he pushed it open, ran through it, and bolted it from within. He waited, all ears, motionless, almost breathless. The footsteps echoed on the other side of the door, the door handle went down and then went up again. Then the footsteps darted down the stairs. He is looking for a second exit and he's going to block them both, Viktor thought. The vestiary, he remembered very well, had a second exit, so he had to get out through the second exit in no time, without leaving any chance for the pursuer to block it. But it was not that easy to find his way through the maze of hangers full of clothes that, suspended above, resembled decapitated corpses obstructing the view in all directions, an array of hangers one after the other, and row after row with little spaces here and there through which one could barely wiggle. But some of these spaces were blocked by shelves full of disorganized piles of worn-out clothes and wigs and masks in a multitude of shapes. He knew, however, where the other exit was, he knew how to avoid all those dead ends, so slowly and tediously he reached the door. He turned the knob. As he pulled it open, he recoiled in terror as the dark void beyond the door like an enormous mouth vomited decapitated heads; a pile of masks and wigs rolled to his feet. Viktor turned back, not knowing what to do or where to go. He found himself ensnared in this vestiary, it seemed forever, in the grip of a nightmare. Not giving much thought as to why, he started wandering desperately in the narrow aisles between the hangers while the dangling clothes seemed to him like people sometime dead and sometime alive, or people who were alive but pretended to be dead, and who were aware that he knew this, to torture him as much as possible because their presence made the situation twice as tormenting. Exhausted and enervated, he stopped someplace and tried to sit down and wait there, though he had nothing to wait for, and then he had an inkling that farther down, among the rows of hangers he had seen a passageway, a door, but not the same one he'd come in. He turned his head, and actually saw a door in that direction. He made for it, full of hope but also anxious lest the door led to nowhere or lest there was no door at all and his eyes had betrayed him, while the door appeared and disappeared behind the rows of hanging clothes until he came in front of it, almost breathless, grabbed the handle, and turned it. The door was unlocked. He was at the top of a narrow flight of iron stairs; on one side was a wall and on the other side, beyond the balustrade, loomed a dark expanse with no end in view. Opposite, a little above him, something was moving, he could hear a muffled rattle, perhaps the mechanism that lifted and lowered the stage curtains, he remembered hazily. Viktor descended the iron stairs to a similarly narrow gallery opening in one end of the dark expanse where he continued to grope in the dark since he could not recognize that part of the building, they have modified it, he thought, they have made changes, of course they would, in the course of his absence of nine years, he had almost forgotten he had been gone for so long, the gallery made a turn, then another and then another flight of stairs, very much like the previous ones, that led down to another open-ended gallery similar to the first one, and then another gallery and another flight of stairs, always the same, and the farther down he went the more the darkness dissipated and he found it much easier and quicker to descend. At last he reached a semidark space in front of a door whence came sounds like music. He opened the door and found himself behind the proscenium on one side of the stage. There some people were peeping at the stage and he could hear the music clearly now. And a voice, a very familiar feminine voice. Viktor came closer and stood behind the curtains. The others did not pay any attention to him, they were concentrating on the performance. From there he could see both Magda singing on the stage, flooded by lights, and a good part of the audience in the concert hall. Their faces were radiant with exhilaration. In no way could exhilaration be kindled by the song, a gush of humdrum sounds, a one-track bland melody with gibberish lyrics. Most likely the show was being performed not only on the stage but also in the concert hall, among the spectators, and was reflected in the clothes they were wearing on this occasion, their jewelry, the uniform frozen smiles on their contented masks. Most likely their exuberance was the outcome of them all at the same time, or was not related to any of them but to something almost intangible, ephemeral that made them hanker after this life, intermingled with the same feeling of estrangement triggered by the marbled radiance of the surrounding new buildings, a haunted space in the city center. It was something that belonged to all those frozen-into-a-smile spectator masks, yet was outside them at the same time and united them into a single being with the voice that came from the stage, singing to the Leader, a unified dumb song of their love for the Leader and the love of the Leader for each one of them. Love, happiness, Magda sang. Because only his love could make you happy because the Leader was the only master of all loves in this life. All loves were dedicated to the Leader. He had taken all loves for himself. He had deprived Viktor Dragoti of the only love he had, he had desecrated it. And Viktor shuddered inwardly, seething with revulsion. He could not remember what happened next, how he found himself on the center of the stage, stiff as a poker as Magda brought her song to an end under the frenzied applause and as the host pointed toward her, smiling at the audience in the concert hall where Viktor found himself seated in three, four, five seats simultaneously, in its center and then the back and then in the front rows; Magda had noticed his presence and was staring at him mesmerized and annoyed and fuming at the same time because the applause died down rather quickly and he was the cause, he was messing up the performance, so Magda exited swearing unintelligibly. Then, alone on the empty stage, Viktor Dragoti turned to the orchestra and asked for a guitar; one of the instrumentalists handed him one, looking at him in confusion and awe. Viktor came to the microphone, opened his mouth as if he was about to swallow it, then started to sing slowly, very slowly, in a low tone of voice, almost in a whisper, an ancient, eerie, savage song, accompanied by a symmetrical, bland melody, a witchlike incantation of a tribe lost in the remote mists at the beginning of time. In the meantime, the frozen-smiling masks in the hall were already dissolving. Suddenly from underneath them, ashen faces full of angst and grief started to emerge, as if overcoming the anguish after the first instant of awakening. Tense, eager to devour every word, every syllable deliberately separated and transformed into an interjection, and every pause of silence between the syllables and sounds. Seated among them he could listen to the breathing, rising and falling and rising again, resounding in the loudspeakers between pauses of silence, while a monster with a multitude of heads and limbs held its breath for a fleeting moment, crumbled in that moment into hundreds of pieces, died as the severed and separate pieces came alive again, and the monster with hundreds of heads and limbs took another shape, revived and then died again and again took another shape and this went on and on and now he could feel it all round him and over the stage onto which some of them had already crept, though in the meantime from above, from the gallery, he could hear a voice shouting, "Out! Get out!"

Now the theater boxes were empty and it was incomprehensible how that voice could have come from above. While down in the parterre the multitudes shifted in waves in an incessant ebb and flow toward the doors, the concert hall remained jam-packed—presumably no one was going out—and at other times they receded and made for the stage, crawling over one another's shoulders and heads, or sitting wherever they could and how they could, spellbound with eyes and mouths wide open, or crawling to and clutching the edge of the stage, jolting and pushing and weighing down on one another in a vain effort to mount.

"Out! Out! Don't listen to the vicious enemy! He is wicked, he is a traitor!"

No one really understood how that voice came from above because the loudspeakers were not working any longer. Viktor started yelling at the top of his lungs, the song was no longer a song, but an outburst of raging voices that somehow continued to vocalize distinctly and persistently a shivering, shuddering story that captivated them all. Viktor felt this, ubiquitous as he was on the plateau and the stage, here and there and everywhere, while all around him the commotion kept growing and the stage and the plateau became one, and the number of those who succeeded in clambering onto the stage became greater, yet they kept pushing and shoving, some even dashed toward Viktor to cut him short, but then greater numbers of people stopped them halfway, hit them furiously, dragged them through the stage toward the curtains, whence they kept trying to come back more and more determined, until one of them, probably the one who had chased Viktor before, yes, it was the same man, the same face, gloomy, dark, pockmarked, and gargantuan, made toward Viktor Dragoti, came within his reach, and almost grabbed him by the arm, not letting him continue to the end, but Viktor promptly poked him in his belly with the head of his guitar and the other bent forward and remained in that position for a moment as if stabbed with a fork, as Viktor dashed off the stage and found himself in a narrow passageway with two doors. He opened one of them, hastily went through, and then ascended a flight of iron stairs that led to a gallery akin to the previous ones, only this one had so many doors, doors, doors. He opened the first one, hurled himself through, and shut it from behind, and at that moment he heard a shriek as though the door itself was shrieking in a woman's voice. Apparently he had entered the dressing room that belonged to Magda, who, though traumatized and dumbfounded, hurried to cover the exposed parts of her half-naked body with whatever she could lay a hand on.

"Shame on you," she scowled irritably, hissing. "How dare you come here after what you did to me."

Viktor was uncertain whether to leave or stay, but since she was keeping her voice down, it seemed that she was not going to drive him away. Numb and speechless he stood at the door, staring at the windowless room overburdened with furniture and clothes thrown in piles all over. Magda was sitting on a stool, with her back against a large mirror.

"You ruined my recital," she spoke again, full of resentment. "How could you do it to me?"

"I'm sorry, Magda," Viktor said at last.

"What was that terrible thing you did, what were those terrible words that came out of your mouth?" Magda screamed, her voice rising in waves. He seized the door handle and was about to leave the room when Magda, smiling coyly, articulated in an undertone, "Don't be afraid, I will not spy on you. Though I can do it, I'm not going to. Can't you see, I'm not that bad after all, you can't despise me." And then purred, "Close the door. Here with me you are safer than anywhere else. I do not sell out my old friends . . . "

Viktor had not been friends with her, on the contrary, he had always given her a cold shoulder. He had even tried to shun and steer clear of her. He somehow vaguely feared this woman, who enticed him with her full thighs, which she was revealing little by little, as if unintentionally.

"Oh, well," he said. "Since you say so . . . "

Viktor made toward her. At that moment Magda stood up, wrapped the robe round her body, and, sidestepping him, went behind a screen.

"I was just changing when you came in," she said, as if she had not noticed anything. "Give me a second, will you, until I change and then we can sit and talk. Take a seat . . . "

Viktor drew up the only stool to a spot where, he thought, he could see her reflection in the mirror, but as soon as he sat down he realized he had made the wrong move. Suddenly running footsteps echoed in the hallway and there were knocks on the closed door.

"Who is it?" Magda shouted.

"Can you open the door?" a man's voice asked.

"No, I can't. Leave me alone!"

"I'm sorry," the voice said.

"You see," Magda whispered as the echo of running footsteps grew weaker and weaker until it faded away. "You are safe, they will not come back . . . "

At that moment, as if frightened by the knocks, Viktor stood up and moved himself a little, to the point where he could see her nakedness reflected in the mirror. She was almost entirely exposed, wearing only her underwear. Viktor could see her ample, luscious curves, a little on the heavy side, but alluring in their dazzling whiteness and suppleness, eager to be sucked up and melt within the obscure male potency.

"Hey, what are you doing?"

Magda had realized his trick at last. She looked at him through the mirror with a playful smile, faking embarrassment, as her hands strove to cover her nakedness, which could not be covered any longer. As Viktor approached her he started to unbutton and remove his clothes hastily.

"Don't, don't, you naughty boy," Magda chirped.

She had no time to say anything else as she pressed her lips to his and then stuck her tongue inside his mouth, their bodies writhing convulsively together. Then they separated for a moment—she took off her underthings as he grabbed a couple of her dresses and threw them on the floor in a bundle and laid her on her back on top of them and made for her open thighs and her belly, which started to bounce. It was a wild sensation, an abrupt awakening of dormant impulses; he yearned to be sucked inside her and to drink interminably at her source of life, her inexhaustible spring. She twisted and turned. She excited and was excited in turn. She was groaning now. It seemed she wanted to give more of herself to him but she couldn't.

"Wait," she said between groans, "Wait . . . be a little more patient . . . let's change position . . . withdraw . . . out . . . "

With some painful effort he withdrew from her and got up, confused. She got up also. Then she turned her back on him, rested her hands on the stool and bent trying to bring her butt as high as possible.

"Come on," she invited him, shivering. "Doggy style, I like it so much . . . "

And they started again. And again she resumed groaning, waving her butt up and down, and he wished this would go on and on but the desire was so burning, he came. He withdrew and collected his clothes to dress. Magda rolled over, drew near him, and kissed him on the lips, but he pushed her slightly as if by accident. Now the exhilaration had worn off and he found her almost repulsive. She tried to embrace him again and gave him a little bite on his uncovered flesh, going down and down.

"Let me put on my clothes." Viktor gave her a little push again.

"Why don't you let me fondle you?" Magda whimpered.

"Let me put on my clothes! I'm in a hurry. I've got to go . . . "

"What, you are not staying with me tonight, aren't we going to make love again?"

"No," Viktor said. "I must go."

"Okay, can we meet later?" Magda pleaded.

Viktor did not say a word. He continued to dress hastily, while she stood in front of him still stark naked.

"So, where can I wait for you?"

"I have no time." Viktor's tone hardened.

"Really, you have no time, eh?" Magda snapped, half angrily and half taunting. "And you have time for the other one, don't you? Because I know you have another one and you want to go and see her."

For a moment Viktor was stunned in bewilderment but managed to collect himself at once.

"Where I go is my business," he said.

"Yes, sure," Magda fired back, "because you did what you liked . . . well anyway I have no right to ask . . . "

Her eyes filled with tears.

"I'm sorry, Magda," Viktor said, "I had no intention of hurting you. But I do have some affairs to take care of and must hurry. Do you understand?"

"No problem," Magda said, wiping off her tears with her fingertips. "Though you are going to meet someone else and refuse me, I cannot refuse you. I will even help you so that you won't fall into the hands of those . . . Wait a minute . . . "

With the attitude of a proud woman who has been hurt and tries not to demonstrate it, she collected her clothes strewn all over the room and started to dress.

"I'll show you the way," she told Viktor in the meantime, "to get out of here without being noticed by anyone . . . You have always disparaged me, I know . . . But you must know, I'm not that bad . . . "

They went out and he followed her through some narrow, austere hallways sprawling one after the other, until they reached a door leading onto the street.

"This way," Magda said, opening the door, "See you . . . "

And she made for the door. Viktor took her hand.

"Thank you, Magda," he said, his eyes lowered with guilt.

"Take care of yourself . . . "

He was left alone. Outside, around him, the street seemed deserted. Now he felt pretty sure nobody was watching him. That he had been under surveillance before was certain, no doubt about it, and all that had happened to him seemed a bad dream from which he had just woken up, and now it was left behind, far, far away.

■ □ ■ □ ■

CHAPTER FIVE

So after nine days in the world of the dead, Ago Ymeri returned among the living for a single day . . .

THE VAST, AWKWARD, MINDLESS, HUMMING CROWD WAS EXITING IN flocks through one of the multilayered doors of the concert hall and pouring down the marble stairs toward the level asphalt ground of the square, drenched by the rain that had just stopped, an obscure mass, with a murky metallic sheen, resembling lava that had just flowed out of deep crevices of the earth and frozen immediately. As he descended the stairs amid people jolting and pushing one another, Bardhyl could pick out some pieces of conversation that drew his immediate attention and piqued his curiosity. He tried not to lose sight of the individual who uttered those words and whose back was the only thing he could see. He followed him more closely, to the sidewalk where the crowd became less dense, and now he could see his half-profile and this was sufficient for him to identify the delicately featured face, like dripping candle wax, of Dhimitër Dakli. Bardhyl decided to speak to him, though they had never been introduced before. But he could not do it right there. He continued to follow him as the other serpentined through the crowd with the desultory movements of a blind man, letting himself be directed by a woman as old as him who most probably was his wife. Bardhyl followed them to the end of the square down to a street where the light ended abruptly, turning the street pitch black as if cut off by an invisible wall. He quickened his steps and drew closer to the old couple. The passersby, few and far between, strode in a hurry and seemed too busy to pay any attention to anybody. The street lamps were lit intermittently and the pale anemic light they produced was imprisoned and sucked in by the black crowns of the trees along the sidewalk. Bardhyl found an opportune moment to address the elderly couple.

"Excuse me, Professor," he said diffidently. "Could you spare a minute . . . ?"

"Sure, yes," Dhimitër Dakli said as he turned around, tilting his face a little upward as the blind do.

"I apologize for annoying you, Professor," Bardhyl mumbled, ". . . with all due respect . . . I heard you a little while ago saying that you had known that . . . Viktor, Viktor Dragoti . . . and I'd like to ask . . . "

"Get lost," the old woman butted in threateningly. "Get lost, leave us alone. Leave the professor alone."

Corpulent and heavyset, with a harsh, gloomy, and spiteful face, in contrast to her frail husband who had an almost childish absentmindedness, she resembled an enraged mother who tries determinedly to protect her child by fending off unexpected dangers and keeping him away from any trouble. Seemingly this made her husband more interested.

"Don't be afraid, woman, let him talk," he said. "His voice tells me he cannot be a bad guy and my ear never leads me wrong . . . Don't pay attention to her," he addressed Bardhyl this time.

She hesitated, and her angry look shifted from Bardhyl to her husband, then in a muted voice she said, "You'll ruin yourself again, you poor wretch, you never learn your lesson."

"Please, what is it you want to say?" the old professor urged.

Bardhyl paused a moment, not knowing where to start.

"I write," he ventured finally. "How to say it . . . I am involved in literature . . . "

"Are you a writer?"

"Better say a neophyte. I dream of becoming a writer."

"That's right, that's right," Dakli murmured thoughtfully. "What's your name, boy?"

"Bardhyl Kosturi."

"I follow the literary magazines . . . she reads those to me, you can guess . . . but I can't recall your name . . . "

Bardhyl felt the shadow of doubt pressing hard on him, emanating not so much from the old man who, so it seemed, spoke freely and with no ill will, as from his wife, who was ready to say *See, it is just like I said, I do not worry in vain*. But she continued to remain silent, a silence as heavy as the words she had uttered a little while ago.

"I do not write to publish," Bardhyl said. "What I write cannot be published."

He had pronounced these words in a single breath and now he was waiting anxiously lest the other would not be willing to continue the conversation.

"Why?" Professor Dakli asked.

"Because I do not want to make any compromises in my writing," Bardhyl said with sincere pride.

"I understand, I understand, I just asked matter-of-factly," said the old man, smiling. "Please, speak up, is there anything you want to learn from me?"

"Of course nothing that can bring you any harm," Bardhyl assured, "though only a very limited circle of loyal friends can read my writings . . . Viktor Dragoti's recital inspired me to write a short story or a novelette, I don't know what . . . but of course, I'll make changes and add to his story and . . . in a word it was a stroke of genius, the beginning, the big bang, the overpressured nucleus from which the world of my creation will be born. As in the ballad, the protagonist will be both Ago Ymeri and Viktor Dragoti at the same time, therefore I wanted to know something about Dragoti's life, especially about what happened to him, why he disappeared, as they say, and also about his character, how you have known him."

After a pause that seemed too long to Bardhyl, overwhelmed with impatience, Dhimitër Dakli alias the Professor, as they called him, thinking in the meantime of the precise words, said at last, "Viktor Dragoti was very outlandish, he was a poet as well as a musician, something unusual in our country. He set his poems to music and then sang them. I daresay he was an Albanian Lluís Llach. It is understandable, a Lluís Llach of Albanian dimensions. But at that time it was possible, or at least he thought so. As a matter of fact, even then, ten years ago, before he left, before he disappeared from here, just like you said, even then no one could express ideas openly, let alone mention the poetry of genuine protest. Nevertheless, unlike you, he thought that a way of compromise could be found, given a certain artfulness, to evade the terrible eye of the monster. And his lyrics, just like his music, encompassed an occult ringing of protest, even when the song was about love, much more so when it was about far-off events, flung back in time, into the past, or to other distant lands, supposedly grieving about their calamity. He was always a fugitive. And then at one point in time he decided to flee the country not only in his poetic rambles . . . "

"Why don't you invite the young man to continue the conversation inside," his wife broke in, as if she wanted to say that now it cannot be helped, we are lost, condescending to invite this man who spoke so dangerously, and whom a while ago she would have not allowed even to utter a single word, into her home.

"I would have invited him with pleasure," said Professor Dakli, "but it is not good for this young man to be seen coming in and out of my home. Since I'm not going to talk for a long time, we can talk on our way to the house . . . "

And they resumed their talk in muted tones, stepping slowly like vanishing shadows in a deserted street that stretched out indefinitely into the twilight.

"After he defected," the professor said, "not only were all his ballads removed from all programs, but the mention of his name became certain ostracism. And as it seems, it was soon forgotten. I'm not surprised your generation does not know him at all. Even older generations that used to listen to his music have already forgotten him."

"I heard his name for the first time today," Bardhyl said. "His music, however, is not quite alien to me. There are some young musicians, I'd say very young ones, but very few of them, who have something of him in their songs. I daresay a great deal. Of course they sing the lyrics in closed circles, in secret hideouts."

"I think they never knew about this similarity, they knew nothing about their forgotten predecessor," the old man said, "or the similarity is quite accidental."

"Possibly," said Bardhyl. "I doubt it, however, they are so much alike. And so very different at the same time."

"His lyrics were as outlandish as his music," the old man continued. "Perhaps this is how they sang in ancient times, in the nebulous beginnings of art when verse and song were one. But today's ballad was extremely bizarre, I don't know if it can be called art. Nevertheless it was powerful and moving. Wasn't it? It triggered such excitement.

Though the music was drawling, dreary. As if it came from the world of the dead. Yes, yes. It almost makes me believe that he died once and now has come back from there, though on the other hand my intellect does not accept the resurrection of the dead."

"Why did he defect?" Bardhyl asked, and promptly provided an answer himself. "Of course, he did not feel free here, because he understood that to compromise his self was impossible."

"So it seems. That news of his defection came as a complete surprise at the time. Not the rumors spread about his murder—such murders at the border were quite common, many did take place— but as it comes out now, this case was a fabrication. I was surprised by his defection because I knew him, and I sensed he was no daredevil. He was quite a commoner, I mean in his daily life, and he was more than prudent. It was quite the opposite with his creativity. He resembled that Baudelairean being, the albatross that seems different up in the air from what it seems on land, it can hardly move around, it can hardly shuffle its poor feet. Apparently life became insupportable here because, as you said, it was impossible for him to keep on trying to compromise with his own self. Or probably he had a premonition that darker times were coming . . . What else can I say to you? This is how I knew the man."

"Thank you very much, Professor," Bardhyl said, "and I apologize for disturbing you . . . "

"No, not at all," Professor Dakli said. "On the contrary, I'm very glad we met. And I rejoice at seeing there are young men like you. I have two more words to say though, before we separate, now we are almost close to my house . . . you do talk to others, don't you?"

"To very few people, whom I trust as I trust myself."

"How come you trusted me? You hardly know me at all and you went so far into . . . "

"You are not a stranger to me," Bardhyl said.

"Despite it . . . "

They had already come to a halt. For a moment they remained in silence. The old man took Bardhyl's hand and squeezed it.

"Take care of yourself," the old professor said. "I am blind but I can recognize the individual I'm talking to straightaway. Probably I can identify him by his voice, or probably by another sense, a sixth sense, who knows. On the other hand, however, I was wrong to get you into this conversation. I can't help it, sometimes I cannot resist temptation. This kind of conversation is tempting for some rare birds, like us . . . "

"When you are tempted then how could I resist?" Bardhyl said.

"My case is different. I know they are not after me any longer. But I did not protect you, that's the bad thing, because you are young and you have your whole life in front of you. Somehow you have to protect yourself. Do not talk to anyone. And forget what we talked about. Forget even all the thoughts in your mind that drive you to talk in ways you should not. No benefit in it, listen to me, I know these affairs too well. And take care of yourself, take care of yourself . . . "

As he said this they shook hands again. Dakli's words still reverberated in Bardhyl's ears after they separated, trailing after him as he walked hurriedly through forlorn and deserted alleys, as if in an effort to escape and sneak past them. Once he arrived home, he rushed into his small bedroom and locked himself in, not even having any dinner. He took a new thick notebook from the drawer, sat at his desk, and started writing.

The Return of the Dead

The Prince of the Underworld, the Lord of the World of the Dead, bored stiff, was languishing in some recess in his cavern. After all, he himself was a beleaguered spirit, condemned to remain in eternal darkness like the spirits sighing in this fathomless funnel, with its neck resembling a narrow shaft, that opened up at the rim of the cavern, as its apex, according to rumors, extended infinitely, eaten away steadily by itself, going deeper and deeper down through darkness and nothingness. He could not recall whether he had ever seen the light, he did not know what it was, therefore he did not know what it meant to see, he could only envision it from the stories of the suffering souls as they reached him from deep down there, mingled with one another, wails echoing in the huge dome of the cavern. He believed he had always been here, since the very beginnings of time, in eternity, and he did not know whether he was blind or had chosen, in some way, from the beginnings of time, from time immemorial, this dark harbor to forget his sightlessness. Keeping his single eye open or shut made no difference to him. Were he to have seen light before, he would have had dreams, as they say all the blind who are not born so do. But he was unable to find out if he had ever slept or not. As if he was between sleep and sleeplessness in a half-dream, half-reality state with no beginning or end in sight. However, time and again he had a vague feeling of waking up for an instant, or rather of being somewhere else in a dream he could not recall. And time rolled by uniformly, nothing occurred aside from some events unvaryingly replicated over and over again and he sensed nothing could ever occur. He was utterly unimpressed by the moans and groans of the toiling souls. He was simply bored, though he was the Prince of the Underworld, the omnipotent Lord of the World of the Dead, and in some way also of the other world where the living souls roamed, because every living soul would be dead in no time. All of them, in a way, were his hostages. He had no idea about the other world where the living souls wandered. Maybe he had created a vague idea though from the stories of those who came from there to stay in his kingdom. Or perhaps he dreamed and afterward forgot about the dream and was left with only a hazy glint. Or perhaps this hazy glint in the confines of the unreachable was not an apparition, it was simply an infatuation, a nostalgic vision of a distant time, gone forever with no return, something lost forever. And this nostalgic feeling was bitter, forlorn, and dismal, and it turned into detestation for everything up there and it filled him with envy for all those that came from there. Consequently it was transformed into a predilection to pry into their anguished and agonized narratives. Still, they could not lift his spirits, and he continued to pry only as a matter of habit, slouching in one of the recesses of his cavern. He was already familiar with all kinds of afflictions and with so many excruciating groans. Once, as he was languishing like that, an abject lamentation rose from the pit of the abyss; he had never heard so much grief, from time immemorial, or perhaps from the very beginning of time, and his tedium was fraught with sorrow.

Go and see why he is lamenting like this, the lord of the dead ordered one of his pages, some huge bat, as huge as the giant birds extinguished at the beginnings of time, the only ones that could see there in the darkness of his realm.

It is nothing my lord, said the page when he came back, *it is someone on his seventh day and he is eating his heart out to return above.*

This is what happens to all of those who are in their seventh day,* thought the Lord of the World of the Dead, the Prince of the Underworld, and yet he had never heard such grieving anguish. He, the Prince of the Underworld, the Lord of the World of the Dead, cowered and was mad at himself for his weakness.

The next day, as he was disconsolately lounging in some recess of his cavern, probably in the same place he had been on the previous day and many days before that, he heard the same thing again, and for an instant he thought the morrow had not come yet, for he could feel the transition from one day to the next, though there was neither sun nor moon nor anything else his only lifeless lightless eye could distinguish in that realm of underground darkness. But no, another day had come and he could still hear the piercing lamentation of the previous day.

This has never happened before, he cried, nearly devastated, and ordered one of the pages to go and fetch the unfortunate wretch. After a while, the flying monster brought him in chains.

Who are you and why are you grieving like this? the Prince of the Underworld asked the shadow.

My name is Ago Ymeri and I am lamenting my cursed luck as I will remain here eternally, said the shadow.

You came by your own choice, for it was impossible for you to live, said the Prince of the Underworld. *And now why are you grieving to go back there? It is the same either down here or up there in the despondent light that leads to blindness.*

Allow me to return there just a single day, said the shadow, *to see the love of my heart for the last time. Yesterday it was my seventh day here and today is the eighth. After my ninth day she will belong to someone else. I have lost her but I just want to see her one more time.*

So, the reason you are eating your heart out is that you want to go back, or do you have another plan you do not want to tell me about? asked the Lord of the World of the Dead, shaking his great head with distrust. He had heard so many times about the mutual passion between the male and female, and he imagined it as the most senseless,

*Footnote by Bardhyl K. in his manuscript: According to an old belief, on the seventh day the dead suffer to come back among the living. Hence the ritual of the memorial day commemorated by the family of the deceased on the seventh day; the forty days ritual comes from the belief that on the fortieth day, the eyes of the dead burst out.

most vain thing, which resulted in them locking their bodies together to give birth then to their offspring, which one day would fall and be tormented to eternity in the dark abysses of his realm.

Allow me to get back there, repeated the shadow, *even for a single day, to see the love of my heart for the last time.*

I don't believe you, said the Prince of the Underworld. Then he fell silent. The silence went on for a long time, as if he had forgotten him. Ultimately he opened his mouth and said, *This is what happens to all the dead. As soon as they reach the seventh day they cry their hearts out to return among the living. It has never happened that somebody continues to suffer after the seventh day, and I have never heard such grief as yours. You shall go.*

So after nine days in the world of the dead, Ago Ymeri returned among the living for a single day, on the same journey he had followed when he left this world, swirling within the successive dark waves that sucked him in and overflowed him at the same time and in their midst he melted away while dying, while he was being conceived by these dark waves as if being awakened and coming out of a dream which was the murky profundity of those waves swirling around him and within him, until he saw himself tossed onto the sandy shore. This is how Ago Ymeri returned among the living and nine years had gone by. He returned from the underground realm of shadows, the eternal abyss of death, to wander only one single day among the living, so he need not fear death, and so fear itself . . .

Since Bardhyl Kosturi was feeling tired and his thoughts had begun to jumble, he stopped writing with the intention of resuming the next morning. But the next morning Bardhyl Kosturi was going to be arrested. The Sigurimi officers who searched his home confiscated this manuscript. Only years and years later after he was released from prison and after many transformations that leveled all the obstacles to the free distribution of books could he find this manuscript and continue right where he had left off, simply with the intention of finishing something he had started a long time ago, as if in this way he could obliterate the prison years, as if in this way he could return something from the bygone years in prison, and not with the intention of publishing it, though its publication had always seemed an unattainable dream, or maybe simply because of this.

■ □ ■ □ ■

CHAPTER SIX

No one really understood how that voice came from above . . .

VIKTOR DRAGOTI MADE A TURN ONTO A BROAD, DIMLY LIT, AND
almost deserted street. By now he had walked through several such
streets and was gradually getting used to the city. He noticed that unlike the square in the center, the other parts of the city had remained
unchanged, yet everything was older, with an abandoned look, the
facades of the houses were grayer, the plaster was peeling off, the wa-
terspouts were deformed or broken, the sidewalks had broken tiles,
and potholes had turned into puddles resembling dead eyes that
became alive occasionally when reflecting some fleeting dim light.
Viktor made a turn onto another street and stopped in front of an
imposing three-story building with a marble portal, like one of those
built by the Italians at the start of the War for the families of average
employees. The window shutters on the left side of the second floor
where Ana used to live were closed and showed no sign of life. Probably there is no one there, he thought, and decided to wait, hoping
she was out and would come back soon. She would come back if she
wasn't home. He lit a cigarette and started to stroll to and fro along
the sidewalk in front of the building. He did not know why and for
what reason he had come here. Perhaps she was with her husband, but
even if he were to find her alone, he was not sure that he would know
her. Considering all the years that had gone by he would not recognize her face even if he had a chance to see her. An irresistible desire
had driven him blindly there, and once there, he could ascertain no
intention for coming. No intention at all, as it seemed. Desperate,

he continued his stroll as if something would come out of his persistence. He waited for some time, possibly an hour or so, but probably much less, he could not tell, when it struck him that Ana might not come at all. They might have moved to another apartment building, he thought. Yet he continued to wait. After all he had nothing else to do. Now he wished for nothing but to see Ana, without giving much thought what he would do afterward. Now his desire to see her seemed to have no connection to his feelings for her, it was something far-off, almost experienced by another being of another kind, an apparition that came to life only inside the ballads he had crafted.

At once, a slow, distorted, otherworldly, blood-freezing lamentation came from above, a wail of flying harpies that became more and more shrill, spreading through the darkening sky, a sirenlike enchantment that grew fainter and all at once started to reverberate from somewhere else, perhaps from the epicenter of the world, while the sky overwhelmed the city, became one with the earth, lights went off abruptly in anguish, everywhere in the streets and the windows, the obscure silhouettes of the buildings and lampposts and castrated trunks and trunkless crowns and everything else around melted in the smooth jelly of the night, a blind shapeless monster that expanded and expanded and only its breathing could be heard, sometimes weak and weary and other times piercing, a sinister augur announcing the end of everything. Then he could perceive remote rumbling noises. A small fire flickered in the distance. Then another. Black shadows swarmed around them as in a wild dance, or as if breaking and smashing objects around. Then pieces of shattered shrieks mingled with a multimouthed scream emitted simultaneously, while other shadows came closer and in heaps scuffled with one another. Wonderstruck and overcome by curiosity, not comprehending what was really going on, or more because he wanted to persuade himself that his eyes were not lying to him, Viktor waited no longer but broke into a run in the direction of the invisible plateau where small fires had sprung up and entangled shadows were swirling, and the nearer he came the more they were transformed into people, breaking windows and poster frames and destroying and burning some huge portraits of some known faces, those of the Leader and some other Politburo members he could distinguish under the fire's glare, and the people swarmed together in groups chanting in unison some incomprehensible slogans and hurled stones and broken marble slates toward some people with helmets and shields and batons who were making steadily in their direction, beating whomever they could, and nobody knew who was hitting whom and who was on this side or that, as flaring fires rose flickering toward the luminous sky, and as right under his eyes the mayhem kept swelling and fuming, the multilimbed lumps of shadows entangled and disentangled relentlessly; some dragged others, listlessly throwing them into vans that drove and disappeared into the dark, but this was not easy and seemed it would come to no end, because no one could realize how those remaining there grew in numbers, because nobody was seen coming from anywhere and they were not many to begin with, but the number remained the same and there was no end to the pandemonium. Viktor Dragoti stopped somewhere in the intersection, looking in wonder and realizing that things were different from how he had left them and much more different from what he thought a couple of hours ago when he arrived, and occasionally he was overwhelmed by the temptation to rush among those people, to break and burn and shoot to death at least one of those robots with helmets and shields, ancient and savage Martians, those shacklers of limb and mutilators of body and soul. He managed to restrain himself somehow and stand by, at the fringe of the darkness, right at the border of the circle illumined by the fires. These are trivial things, he thought, though they are faint hints of bigger events that will follow eventually. He had no time to wait. And it was worthless to join the dance, since right now he could do something more valuable, an unprecedented feat. He could not make a decision, though, for he did not know where he was, isolated in a somewhat unknown world. And again he was lured by the vortex that whirled furiously in front of him in that intersection, the temptation was so enticing, yet he managed to resist, until at last he decided to go and find one of his old friends, talk to him and understand how matters stood, and then decide what to do, so that his journey should not have been wasted. He decided to ask somebody who knew how matters stood, he decided to ask his old friend Dhimitër Dakli, who had been so close to him that once he told him, you, Viktor, are a safe stronghold where I can find refuge at any time, and Viktor thought Dhimitër Dakli was a refuge for him, too, out of reach of imminent danger, he lived somewhere near there, and despite the darkness Viktor would find the place unmistakably, even blindfolded.

In a little while he found himself in a muddy space between the apartment houses. On all sides he was surrounded by rows of similar buildings, he could not tell one from the other, and could not remember in which one Dhimitër Dakli's apartment was. Somehow he had the strange feeling that it was in each one of them. He went into one of the apartment buildings, ascended a flight of stairs, stopped in front of an apartment door, and rang the bell.

"Who is it?" he heard the voice of Dhimitër Dakli's wife.

"It's me, Viktor," he said in a low tone of voice, almost in a whisper.

"Viktor who? Who are you looking for?!"

"Is this the Dakli family?" he asked hesitantly.

"No, you have the wrong address," said the voice laced with some annoyance.

Viktor stood confused in front of the door, as he heard whispers and words he could not distinguish coming from inside, uttered by another voice, which he recognized as that of Dhimitër Dakli. Viktor was about to leave when the door opened. He turned back and went in. In a narrow room, illuminated by weak candlelight flickering on worn furniture and on a window covered by old fabric because of the enforced blackout, Viktor was standing in front of his friend, just as he had stood nine years ago and many times before that and he felt like believing his absence had only been for a short instant, he had just taken a nap, always present there, transfixed outside the flow of time.

"As you can see, I'm back," Viktor started the conversation. "I returned from the place of no return. Just for a single day because I have to be there again tomorrow before dawn . . . "

"What are you talking about?" said the other. "Do you mean that the legend you recited tonight on the stage is true? That what you declaimed there really happened to you?"

"Yes," Viktor said, "more or less."

"You're kidding."

"You don't trust me?" Viktor said. "I can neither lie nor hide anything from you. I have come from over there, the world of the dead."

Professor Dakli shook his head with a faint gesture, staring at him. Probably he thinks I'm insane, Viktor thought, considering that he was present at the performance tonight. He faked a bitter smile but did not budge.

"How have you been?" he tried to change the flow of conversation.

Now it was the old man who faked a bitter smile while his stare became hazy.

"Since you left," he said, "I spent most of my time in prison. This time it was because of a letter I wrote to that man-eater who is leading the country. Even if I had not written it I would have been thrown into prison anyway. I can even say I knew it was going to happen, foreseeing the coming events, and when I was losing my sight I thought to use what was left to write that letter, at least to give vent to my feelings so that I could deserve prison and feel better about myself rather than wait for it peacefully. Do you understand? The writing accelerated my blindness and it wrapped me up as if in a black veil upon finishing the letter, as I was resting after the painful strain. I do not regret it though because, as I told you previously, they would have thrown me into prison no matter what. Disastrous events were brewing, a feverish witch hunt started with the purge of a couple of high propaganda officials, and then gradually spread to all walks of life and to all categories of people. The Gaz vehicles roamed like hungry wolves, arresting people in their homes, while almost every week prison vans arrived at the camp one after the other to bring twenty or thirty new prisoners at once. As a matter of fact, those who had been in prison before were the most desirable prey of this hunt. Actually this time it was much harder for me because the first time I was young and still strong healthwise. I thought I would not come out alive. Yet I did, but I contracted an incurable disease that will soon bring me to the grave."

"What do you mean?" Viktor interrupted.

"Yes, yes, I have cancer," said Dhimitër Dakli, lowering his voice so that his wife, who had already gone to the next room, could not hear him. "I know by now . . . Even if I could live longer, what could I do? I feel sorry only for my wife, she will be left alone. She has already learned about this but does not want to believe. She thinks it exists only in my head. It was half the harm when after I was released from prison they did not deport us but let us live our last days in our home. We are also given a pension sufficient just to make ends meet. I cannot teach foreign languages anymore not because I am blind, I could manage, but because people have become more cautious and do not dare take private lessons with people like me."

The old man paused. Then silence fell for a time and he noticed that Viktor was about to say something when Dhimitër Dakli's wife stepped into the room with coffee on a copper tray full of medicine bottles. Viktor waited until she left the room and until Dhimitër Dakli, with the same bitter smile on his face, took one pill from each of three or four bottles.

At last Viktor said, "Please listen. I came to take a piece of advice from you. In a matter of hours I will go back there where I belong, among the dead. You probably do not believe me, or probably you think I am crazy, but I fear nothing, I am already lost, so before I go back there I want to do something, I am ready to do anything against this government. I do not know where to start, whom to contact, or what would be most fruitful. In a word, I do not know the situation . . . "

"Your words make sense," said Dhimitër.

Viktor Dragoti said no more as he stared at the old man's lips in confusion, his impatience bordering on anxiety.

"Whether you have been where you say or not," the old man went on, "is of very little importance, since as you do not fear death you fear nothing in this world. Or probably you have gone so far as to realize this world we live in does not differ from the other one, and in some way I daresay I believe you came from over there and that you are going back. This is how I felt when I was listening to the ballad you sang tonight, and I assume this is what the audience also felt. However, it could not captivate their souls. You should not be deceived by the false appearance of things. It was only an outburst of the moment and most of those present in the concert hall, almost all of them, as soon as they exited, forgot everything they heard, saw, and felt, and will even be afraid to recall it. And the result of this event will be to the benefit of the Sigurimi, enabling it to pick out some more candidates for prison, the ones who appeared to be the most unrestrained, and very soon, I think, they will be in shackles. It would have been better if you hadn't done what you did and basically any attempt you may make will be futile."

"I am so surprised," Viktor said vehemently. "A little before I came here I witnessed some events that indicate people are awakening.

Probably by now they have been contained, but a while ago I think you heard the commotion outside. It took place very close by, in a number of city zones simultaneously, which made it difficult to understand where it originated, and it spread in waves. It was an uprising in miniature. It was wonderful. People did not care, they did not fear anything anymore, and I could not recognize them. This is all, when they have no more fear, as soon as it starts then everything finds a way . . . Of course it is not easy, it must be a far-reaching and organized act . . . But as far as I could see they have started to get organized . . . "

The teasing smile that wandered wearily on the lower part of Dhimitër Dakli's face turned into a grimace. This time though, he followed Viktor to the end.

"You think I am completely isolated from the rest of the world," he said after Viktor stopped talking. "But I follow all the events and I know all of what you already told me, as everybody else does, though I am blind and I live isolated. I know very well, just as everybody else does, that the clashes in the street, like the one you saw tonight, are nothing but prevarication, simulated incidents, fabricated by the government under its direct care and ordered by the highest officials. These performances, because they are performances pure and simple, are organized as you can imagine by the Sigurimi on the occasion of any official celebration, such as the one today, to finalize the Week of the Leader, in celebration of his birthday. This is a kind of occasional training, so as to nip in the bud any attempt at an imagined uprising, or it is, I daresay, a kind of a test for the government to prove to itself that it is always invincible. It is a show pure and simple, with actors and decor, a masquerade because not only are the clashes between the people and law enforcement staged but all that is broken and destroyed and burned as well, everything to be destroyed, is put in special places a little before the show begins and nothing else can be touched."

"What about those who are arrested?" Viktor asked. "What happens to them? I saw all those people being dragged and thrown into police vans. Or is their detention part of the play as well?"

"Precisely," said the old man scornfully. "They release them the next morning."

"Aha," said Viktor, and then asked, "Isn't this staging, this occasionally repeated show fraught with the potential for consequences opposite from what those in power expect? Does it not represent a dangerous example, reminding the people that they can rise in revolt, or at least that the leaders can be desecrated and such things, something which they could never imagine otherwise, or dare dream of, as you said . . . In a word, don't those above think that people, just like children who learn through play, can one day start for real?"

"Oh, this can never happen," Dhimitër Dakli said, as he shook his head cheerlessly. "The people who participate in such events are pre-assigned . . . actually they are not selected on the basis of some special political trust toward the government, on the contrary, they are ordinary people, randomly selected, but selected anyway, and when the alarm goes off, they immediately take to the streets and, punctual and blind as somnambulists, each one of them and all together play their respective parts. They are as if programmed for this kind of job . . . Not only them, but everybody is programmed in some way, each and every one of us is something between a sleepwalker and a robot. All, in some way or another. Even I, though I was in prison and my ideas are what they are, even I have remnants of something in common with the power from the time when the movement that gave birth to this power began . . . Well I was speaking about the performance, the show. As I said, even the detention is part of it, it is the epilogue, the crowning of it all. By the next morning, by the time they are released they have forgotten everything, as if nothing ever happened. I don't know if there are the same performers each time or others, or a combination of both. The effect, though, is the same both on the participants and the onlookers, because this show acts as a kind of purification, a kind of exorcism. A kind of controlled duplication of the dream, I daresay, so that they do not dream of things they must not. Concurrently, in the eyes of the government this is a tour de force, a self-conviction of the power and strength it cherishes and propagates at all times, persuading the people of it and seeing it reflected in their obedience. In sum, such repeated simulations of its overthrow during celebrations assist its perpetuation and in some way prolong its life."

"But the . . . they above?" Viktor asked at last, contorting painfully. "How are things going in their midst? You said there were purges, didn't you? Is it possible that in this commotion somebody else more lenient will come into the leadership and so changes could start gradually?"

"Don't pin your hopes on them, Viktor." The old professor waved his hand in front of his face in an effort to shoo away a spurious apparition. "Such hopes captivate a man when he feels completely powerless, for example when he prays to an unknown deaf deity. I know those above too well to be allowed the luxury of hope. True, some purges have taken place among them, and, as I can sense, others will soon follow. The great monster is making preparations to die and in the meantime is trying to pave the way for his successor, no one knows who. Whoever comes, it will be the same, perhaps worse. You know I was one of the forefathers of the movement and I know it too well, I know it in its origins. More than a movement, it can be called a frenzied downhill course aiming always forward, always forward, crushing under its feet anybody who dares try to change its course. Now it is too late for any of them to get such ideas in their heads. Those who aspired to another course were thrown out in the first days and months, the first years at most, and the later purges more and more resemble the fight of robbers over loot."

Then the lights came on. Everything around seemed naked and frozen for a moment. Dhimitër Dakli was silent as if quite defenseless.

"Oh, light is back on," Viktor said.

"Yeah," said the old man.

"So you can feel it though you do not see it?" Viktor was surprised.

"Precisely."

"And on the other hand you do not feel the slightest hope, the slightest ray of hope . . . "

"Precisely," repeated Dhimitër Dakli. "Not because I am blind. Though from the time I went blind I have been able to see more clearly."

"You have always been able to see what the eye couldn't see," Viktor admitted.

"I don't know," said the old man. "Now, though sightless, I see better than before."

"And what do you advise me finally?" asked Viktor.

"Absolutely nothing," said the old man. "Only watch over yourself. Probably even this piece of advice is out of place because it comes a little too late. You have already put yourself in so much danger, especially for what you did at the concert and by coming here."

"I have considered everything," Viktor Dragoti said. "No doubt your apartment is monitored."

"I don't know," said the old man, "probably not, because it is not necessary. I have the impression that those above, those who are at the pinnacle of power, monitor all my conversations and even what I think without the need of any medium, just as I can penetrate their minds, as if it is a ubiquitous mind."

"I do not understand you," said Viktor, flabbergasted.

"I do not understand myself sometimes," Dhimitër Dakli said. "Anyway, every now and then when I talk to somebody or even to myself, as my words or thoughts travel on forbidden trails, I get the impression that somebody is wiretapping me from inside, somebody I myself have conceived unintentionally in my feverish endless efforts to penetrate the layers of state power. This numbs my tongue, dulls my thinking, but then the evil is done, and when I am reminded of this it is already a bit too late, because of course, I like such conversations, whenever I can, and it is difficult to avoid them. And the unknown within me that monitors me lies dormant and revives only when it does not want me to talk any further. What is worse, I do not harm myself—there is nothing that can harm me now, because they are fed up with my flesh and blood already, I am nothing more than an unburied corpse—but unwillingly I bring harm to others, to those who have not yet known fear and who dare think and come to me in good faith. Maybe this is the reason why they did not deport me but left me here, in the center of Tirana."

"Maybe it is not exactly like that," Viktor Dragoti said, astounded by what he heard, all of this seeming to him like the unbelievable caprice of an overworked brain in the grip of desperation.

The old man did not speak; his lightless eyes were fixed on Viktor's eyes as his face remained distorted by a smirk that made him look older and reduced in size. What he said earlier cannot be right, Viktor thought. He likes to torture himself, secluded as he is in this darkness. He was about to dispute what they had talked about when Dhimitër Dakli, immersed as he was in his own thoughts, said, "Actually I can see a ray of hope, far, far away. The destiny of this country will change eventually and then abundant prosperity will come to it as to no other; only in this way will the enormous agony and misery we have suffered and are still to suffer be paid off. The turn of destiny will come eventually because the world itself, nature itself is conceived in this way, inclined toward an impeccable balance, the foundation of our very existence, without which humans would be deprived of the feeling of justice and righteousness and suffering from its occasional violation. But it is a very distant future, at a dreamlike distance. But for now and for a long time to come I see only darkness. Now nothing stirs, nothing will change. Told in the language of your ballad, we are all locked inside Polyphemus's cave and time has come to a standstill. Or I daresay this dreamlike future is beyond immortality for us. Then yes, everything will change suddenly and instantly, but today we can do nothing to bring it nearer or prepare for it, because the connection between the present and that future does not exist, because there is a terrible abyss between them and in its dark void every endeavor and attempt we could make today would fall and vanish in it. Therefore, once more, you can do nothing but take care of yourself."

"What can they do to me?" Viktor said. "I am dead already."

"I am dead, too," Dhimitër Dakli said. "I have nothing to enjoy in this life, I am dragging through my last days in lethargy. And I do nothing, not because I am scared but because whatever I could do would be pointless. So in this life I have nothing left but the miserable seat of an onlooker and occasionally that of a chatterbox who brings harm to others by accident. Your situation differs from mine because you were down there and came back. I assume an immense regret brought you back. Therefore I advise you to take care of yourself so that they do not send you back before you make all efforts to release yourself from it."

He had already sensed what Viktor was contemplating, what was seething within him.

As if to change the subject, Viktor asked him, "Do you recall more than nine years ago, there was a girl named Ana, who came occasionally to take French lessons, I think? I met her here several times, so I assume she came here frequently."

"I remember you asked me the same question then," Dhimitër said, "and I told you that she was engaged to the nephew of one of the Politburo members."

"Yes," Viktor said. "We had exchanged only some glances when I fell for her. Because of her those were the happiest days of my life. Maybe since my childhood. When I learned she was engaged to be married soon, I was overwhelmed with despair. Everything seemed empty and gloomily miserable, because everything reminded me of Ana. I felt I forgot everything about my previous life, the people, the streets, the air. It might sound strange to you but this is what drove me to the decision to defect."

"Oh, crazy you," Dhimitër Dakli screamed through painful guffaws. "Oh, crazy you. And I thought you wanted to leave because you could not support the bondage any longer, that you were in search of freedom . . . "

"That was another reason," Viktor murmured, blushing, while the harshness of the other's voice made him feel ill at ease. Then his speech became more determined: "That was another reason, but it was that madness that drove me to the decision to defect, for me it was more powerful than reason . . . Do you have anything to tell me about Ana?"

"Did you love the girl that much?" Dhimitër asked, flabbergasted and timid at the same time for having embarrassed the man. "Well, I'll tell you what I know. After I was released from prison, I met her several times at the oncology hospital, she's still working there. Then, one time, we met in the street and she stopped and talked to me. I thought she could allow herself the luxury of this courage because she was untouchable because she was the wife of the nephew of a Poltiburo member. But she told me they had divorced a long time ago. And she took good care of me at the hospital where not all doctors are ready to serve those who are considered enemies. Apparently she is a very courageous woman; she is fearless but I have the impression it is her desolation that drives her, because spiritually she has given in. She lives a secluded life and if religion were allowed she would be a nun in a monastery, this is what she told me. That is it, my friend. What else can I say?"

A moment later Viktor Dragoti was pacing briskly along the street. Hurriedly he raised his head two or three times, staring at the dark dome of the sky, apparently in search of something among the dense, rugged clouds, where a dim and grayish light flickered here and there, as the moon was nowhere to be seen, nor was the sun; he would not be able to see the sun in his last day-night in this world that bore such a resemblance to the world of the dead, with never a glimpse of the sun nor the moon.

■ □ ■ □ ■

CHAPTER SEVEN

The vault of the world of the dead would rupture . . .

THE EARTH OPENED UP SLOWLY. A CONVOY OF BURNISHED BLACK
caskets, the automobiles of the Politburo members, ascended from its
gaping depths and spilled out. Hell yes, thought the Minister of the
Interior with the same feeling of soothing gratification that warmed
him whenever he met with the Leader, as his automobile came out
last. But now such gratification was mixed with a certain restlessness.

"Take us to Villa Seven," he ordered the driver as they emerged
from the underground.

Unlike the other vehicles, the automobile of the Interior Minister
snaked through several streets in the Bllok and headed toward Martyrs of the Nation Boulevard, deserted at that time of evening, a desolation that had become more pronounced by the trees lining the sidewalks with their branches pruned back to the trunks. After making a
turn into a side street somewhere and then following a wider street
that ran parallel to almost the entire length of the boulevard, the automobile accelerated, only to slow down a little later as it made a turn
into a labyrinth of quiet short alleys, and then carved several turns
through them, pulling up at last in front of a gate with wrought-iron
bars that led to the front yard of a two-story villa, its facade covered
with ivy leaves and surrounded by pine trees that looked like lonely,
reticent, unusual guests from a far-off world. The bodyguard got out
of the car, unlocked the gate, and pushed it open. The car drove into
the front yard and came to a halt at the main entrance of the building. A dim light coming from somewhere in the building flickered

through the translucent glass door. This opened and at the entrance the villa caretaker appeared, a well-groomed and delicate middle-aged woman, who upon hearing the arrival of the automobile had rushed to welcome the minister. She greeted him with a bashful smile and mumbled a few words as the minister walked past her and went in, not even deigning to throw her a glance. She followed and dashed to the light switch in the entrance hall, turned it on, and then, still diffident and irresolute, helped him with his overcoat.

"Now you can go home," the minister said to her.

"At your orders," the caretaker replied, in a muted voice that failed to hide her anxiety and fear.

The bitch, the minister thought, she is willing. He eyed her from head to toe before he made for the upper level. She is not bad, she's even worth it, he thought as he ascended the stairs and shot a glance at her breasts from above. I'll try this dish one of these days. It's worth it, she looks hot, the slut. He perceived a certain hidden yet intentional fascination on her part, secretly unfaltering yet fearfully held back by the power vested in him. He had sensed this before but he felt something inexplicable within that made him hesitate and put off the affair till a later date, the next time, and it had always been like this during the three or four times he had come to the villa in the last few months since she had started work there, replacing the trusted old caretaker. This one, though a female, and females by nature being more gossipy than males, must be trustworthy since his bodyguard had found her. Yet there was something sinister about this woman, something alluring and repulsive at the same time. His bodyguard, what was his relation to this female? Perhaps she is his mistress, he thought dispassionately, surprisingly with no envy whatsoever, even with certain relief, a feeling he had never had for those under him, as he came to the landing and then continued slowly through the semi-darkness of the hallway. In fact, when he dismissed her, from the corner of his eye he saw some exasperation fall on the bodyguard's s face. Hell yes, he thought, and stepped into one of the rooms opening onto the dimly lit corridor. He turned on the light and went to the intercom at the desk, pressed one of the buttons and transferred the line to his home. Then he switched on the small mushroomlike lamp by the telephone and turned around to switch off the chandelier he had lit a moment ago. The minister crossed his hands behind his back and started his usual pacing in the room, while his silhouette, an impenetrable, omnipotent jinni of the fairy tales, glided over the walls, casting shadows that became more resolute as they shrank and lost their contours as they enlarged. Hell yes, he said to himself again. Now he knew all too well where Viktor Dragoti was headed, for the time being let us call him so, because this is what the dimwitted Dhimitër Dakli also believed. But Dhimitër Dakli's impaired judgment was in no way to be trusted. The minister himself had very much wanted him to be the one he was not, so that he could nail Ferhat by accusing him of concocting a fraudulent murder for the purpose of sending his trusted man to his patrons overseas. But he, the Minister of the Interior, had seen with his very own eyes Viktor Dragoti's corpse washed ashore by the waves, moreover the forensic experts had unmistakably identified the corpse, and yet there were a few things that made one believe the nameless unknown individual was none other than Viktor Dragoti, the leads that kept growing in number reinforced this belief, especially the commotion at the concert when many had recognized Viktor Dragoti by his appearance, his voice, his music, everything coincided with what the lunatic in the madhouse said, and with what Dhimitër, the other lunatic whom we let go free, believed. What had taken place in the concert hall was sheer madness and hundreds of crazy people can be trusted less than a single lunatic, the minister thought, trying to ward off a shade of suspicion that a dead man could return among the living, as he had caught himself thinking more than once that day, almost to the point of believing it could happen. That was the reason why he had named the unknown man after Viktor Dragoti and he wondered how he could do that, was it because he wanted him to be that person and nobody else, well let him have this name for the moment, there is nothing bad in calling him by this name, the more so because all those who met him did so. Well, Viktor Dragoti told his friend that he was going to meet with Ana, and yes, it was true, he was going there. And as for the other thing he told his friend, that he had never dated Ana Gremi, just an exchange of glances, this could not be swallowed. Bullshit. Very strong old ties must have existed between them since he was going to meet her. Hmm, Ferhat, now you are my target. As it turns out, she is the big spider. She has been waiting for him just like Penelope weaving her interminable cloth day and night, staying faithful to him for so many years, disregarding the powerful suitor, Ferhat's nephew, whom she divorced to wait for the other one. Great love, I'm dying for you and other such nonsense. But of course, this was not all. We are in pursuit of that Viktor Dragoti every step he takes, every moment on his way, we'll let him in and let them converse about their dark affairs and even fornicate if they feel like it, but afterward during interrogation we'll make them pay through the nose and make them render an account of what they talked about, what instructions they received and exchanged during this time, we'll give them time and we won't need to hurry to apprehend them, no, we must not hurry, just like the Leader, who never hurried and was allowing this dangerous being coming from hell to graze freely for a time, though it is impossible for him to have come from there but it is the same as if he had come from there, this dangerous being who does not know fear, this frightful being who can do anything as a result, a dead man who defies death, how can we let him loose and not apprehend him as soon as possible and throw him into some remote dungeon from where he can never return as no one can from hell, he has to be thrown there the sooner the better. As always, however, the Leader was prudent, patient, and farsighted, and this yielded better results, as always, as if he knew, to some extent he did know, that this Viktor Dragoti would meander and then meet with Ana Gremi, the former wife of Ferhat's nephew, just as I would have ordered him to do or just as the Leader would have predicted. He would go there were he to have enough time, and that is why he let him have enough time to make it much easier for me to entrap Ferhat, and I'll be more prudent and give him time, let them stay together for a while, until they connect the threads we need, let him enter her apartment, it is not necessary to apprehend him at the moment he gets there, though this is sufficient evidence, let him go in and fall deeper and deeper into the ditch, into the black tangled spider web, then we break in, at the moment he mounts her, at the onset without giving him time to finish, or no, better at the moment of his ejaculation as he melts in her cunt, or maybe the best is to let them enjoy one another until dawn, let them scuffle once more sleepily and then we break in, at the moment of his exhaustion within the black spider web, right at the roots of the calamity threatening to smite us by means of the poisonous threads that protract and protract invisibly, but once we take hold of the roots we will be able to reach wherever they have spread, to whomever and however far, high, and low, even to Old Nick, Ferhat himself, because there is no other but him. The divorce between Ana Gremi and his nephew must have been one of his fabrications. Since he wanted her to be free for other affairs when the time was ripe as it is right now. No wonder their unexpected divorce went so quietly and so unnoticed. According to rumor, Ferhat had allegedly summoned Ana to persuade her not to divorce his nephew but now it appears they must have come to an agreement about something else. For that is the reason Ana Gremi did not suffer any consequences afterward, that must be the real reason, and not that Ferhat spared her and did not harm her in a gesture of leniency and not revenge. No one is buying this, Ferhat, the Interior Minister sneered. At that instant he wondered why he hated Ferhat so much. More than once during that day, which marked the threshold of Ferhat's downfall, his doom, the minister returned to the beginning, the War, when they were the best of friends, more than brothers, so close that many confused their names and feats. Returning to that beginning, the Interior Minister thought for a moment that his present hatred of Ferhat, his attempt to bury him, was unbelievable, a nightmare. What would he have done then, during the War, had he imagined that matters would come to this, the minister asked himself, trying to find out how his abhorrence for Ferhat had started. And his hatred for some others whose graves both he and Ferhat had dug. With Ferhat and others who would be buried in other graves, all of them, one after the other with the exception of the Leader. Obviously, now that the Leader and I know so many things, we can never swear there are no traitors among us, we can trust no one, but myself and the Leader, how easily we trusted then, and for us it was not easy to open our eyes. It seemed unbelievable when for the first time, together with the Leader, we uncovered the first traitor, we were so confused we started to be afraid even of ourselves, but the unfathomable hatred for the infidelity of the traitor helped us to pull ourselves together and bring back our trust in ourselves, the notion that we were not like him, that we were united by loyalty to the Leader, which became stronger, nurtured by hatred and by the trust of the Leader in us, and grew after this test, it nourished us with greater loyalty, trust, and love for each other, but then when another more perfidious traitor, more unbelievably, was exposed in our midst, we got more confused and started to fear more for ourselves, but we were not like him and the boundless hatred toward the traitor and the loyalty to the Leader who helped us uncover the traitor and his trust in us made our relations stronger and our love for each other grew so powerful that when another traitor was uncovered and then another and then another, we hated them the more because we had loved them so much, and our love and trust were transformed so many times into such intense hatred against infidelity that it became impossible for us to tell if we really loved each other, if we were the closest of friends and could sacrifice our own lives for the sake of the others, or if we hated and wanted to destroy each other, a double, dual, distorted, and distorting feeling, suspicion and subjugation and pleas for mercy in silence and humiliation, an unbearable humiliation that stealthily, inconceivably, and blindly converted into bitter and extreme abhorrence as an escape from feeling powerless and mutely subjugated, from languishing at the mercy of the others, humiliated by them. This old abomination of Ferhat, God knows how and for what reason it had started, might have started long ago or quite recently, probably when he sensed that he was threatened by Ferhat, who was in a slightly higher position than himself, higher than the Minister of the Interior, but this could not be the case, how could the idea of being threatened by Ferhat ever cross his mind, as if it were not him but someone else who sensed this, as happens to people in dreams when they see themselves as outsiders, as another person, and then forget the experience as soon as they come out of the dream. Neither Ferhat nor anybody else could do anything to him for as long as he was loyal to the Leader and enjoyed his trust and would become the Leader himself after this Leader and after having blown Ferhat's head off, and as he pondered perplexedly about all this and why he hated him so much, he was shocked just as much as when for the first time he felt he abhorred him, and realized from that moment on that he had hated him all along, he did not want to drive Ferhat to ruin and blow his head off for the sake of taking the position of the Leader instead of him, as he had doubted so many times whenever he wondered why it happened with his old friend, but he, the Minister of the Interior had an intuition that had never failed him, as if he knew from the very beginning that the day would come when Ferhat would become a traitor and worse than that, so all that drifting apart, aggravation, stringent hatred were not without reason, they were still going strong even to this day, even at the last moment before he spoke to the Leader, when everything was decided about Ferhat once and for all, and he the Minister of the Interior again and again wondered why it happened to his old friend, what should he have done then during the War had he imagined, however vaguely, that things would come to this, and therefore tried and did his utmost to save his friend, for whom he would have given his own life back then, he was more than a brother to him, but he was more than a traitor, he would have done his utmost were he to do anything and still be loyal to the Leader and the Party and the people but today's events and Ferhat's acts hiding behind them spoke for themselves and did not give him a chance to speak up, the Leader had foreseen with his usual perspicacity everything that would happen, everything his minister intuited, and he had intuited what the Leader had in mind, and thus his conscience was clear, despite Ferhat's elimination. Hell yes. He sat on the large couch beside the writing desk, tired of his long pacing about the room and the overload of that eventful day that rolled at reckless roller-coaster pace, he needed to rest because he still had work to do that day, that day-night with no end in sight. Though tired, he sprang to his feet, urged by an inexplicable inner drive, and went to one of the windows and peeked through the heavy reddish curtains, his gaze falling on the dark pine treetops behind the window. They reminded him of a scientific film he had seen long ago, hmm, about some nerve cells that branched out like trees, yes the old Greek word for which they were named meant "tree," and these sequences mixed together with a forgotten early dream that came back to his mind in the image of a huge black mushroom, and some black bugs hovering over and under the mushroom cap, perhaps in a race to chase away other bugs appearing and disappearing in the twinkling of an eye between the mushroom gills, which started to drip murkiness that coagulated and then drip drop, drip drop turned to a viscous poisonous black liquid and the bugs between the mushroom gills got stuck there and were caught amid painful flames, but it was not the other bugs that aroused and instigated the mushroom because a resounding voice uttered in old Albanian something that meant that all bug movements were determined by the mushroom itself, though it might not be the case, because all of this was an entertaining game of destiny and that was all. He woke up from his slumber and found himself leaning on the large couch by the writing desk, his slightly parted legs stretched out, and noticed he had not reached the window and had not budged from his seat at all. He looked at his watch. He had dozed off for only a couple of minutes, it was already going on eight o'clock and he thought Magda was a little too late. Though tired and not able to deal with her, such a delay made him nervous and he decided to call and tell her to come as soon as possible. He reached the desk, raised the receiver and dialed the number hurriedly.

"Hello! . . ."

On the other end Magda picked up the phone. She purred languidly.

"Hello! . . . Oh, is it you, my darling?"

"Yes, it's me," the minister said. "Did you forget about tonight?"

"What are you talking about," Magda responded, "only that . . . please, darling . . . don't get angry . . ."

"What happened?"

"Nothing," Magda said, "only I am tired, very tired . . ."

"Are you feeling depressed?"

He remembered what happened during the recital and thought that was the reason why she felt cheerless and depressed.

"Depressed?" Magda shrieked, faking surprise. "Why?"

"About the concert," the minister said.

"Ah, yes," Magda said, taking a deep sigh. "I was a little annoyed, of course."

Between sighs, however, her voice had a cheerful tone. Nobody can understand a female, the minister thought.

"Why didn't you call me, at least to tell me you were not coming?" he asked Magda, trying to convey a certain threat in his reproach.

She paused for a second, as the minister waited curiously to hear what she had to say about this.

"Well," Magda said, "my father is not here, he went to see my uncle, and I was afraid to call myself, I thought your phone might have been connected to your home and that somebody else might pick it up . . ."

"Aha," the minister said coldly. "In a word, you are not coming tonight?"

"I am so tired, darling. I told you, I am exhausted. Don't get angry with me, darling, it's not good . . ."

The minister hung up and did not hear how her excuse ended. Yet he was not angry. He even felt better that she was not coming. Not because he was tired and not able to deal with her. In fact there was something new, an unknown exciting pleasure in her defiance, she said no to him for the first time, the minister almost felt flattered that this woman was disobeying this single time. Anyhow he felt more masculine with a disturbed overpowering strength, yet less fulfilled at the same time. Unexpectedly the image of the other one, the caretaker of the villa, with her sensual fawning and the annoyance on his bodyguard's face, flashed in front of him. He must have kept her, he said to himself, almost pretty sure that the bodyguard had violated his order this time and he wished it so. Let me see what they are doing. As he descended the stairs he visualized, trembling, how he would catch them right at the moment when they were on top of each other, then he would yell at one and then at the other, his bodyguard first, giving him a kick in the butt at the same time, and then the caretaker, he still did not know what he was going to do to her until he'd shown her what it means to be powerful, and she'd feel the power, being in his arms for a moment, nestling him between her thighs, and the next moment she'd again be reduced to a miserable being just as she had always been, and even much more so since she'd have known power and he'd behave as if nothing had ever happened between them. To take her again later when she'd lost all hope. Stepping noiselessly through the narrow twisting service hallways, his ears pricked to catch the slightest sound, he came to a door behind which he could hear groans and moans and flung it open. Illuminated by the light coming from the hallway he saw the rear end of a male in up-and-down motion between two wide-opened thighs showing under a black skirt raised above a white belly, he saw them both lying on a lumpy bed, the caretaker and the bodyguard on top of her. The bodyguard froze as if experiencing a cramp and then recoiled to hide his naked body parts, confused what to cover first, managing at last to stand up and pull up his pants with the fly still open and the belt hanging like a dead lizard. The minister turned the light on.

"What are you two doing here?" he shouted dreadfully.

The caretaker receded to the border of the bed. Her thighs had already disappeared.

"I'm sorry Comrade Minister," the bodyguard stammered, with his head down and the face of a mortified child.

The minister looked at him and then at the caretaker. Crouching, cowering, she was reduced to another unattractive being. A miserable old woman, almost a hag. The room had a heavy cadaverous smell.

"It is your fault," the minister turned to the bodyguard. "First, you forced her to stay, violating my strict order. Second, your job is to protect me and not fuck somebody else's wife. Third . . . aren't you ashamed of yourself . . . shame on you that . . . that . . . "

"I am so sorry, Comrade Minister, I won't do it again . . . "

"You, go home to your husband," the minister said to the caretaker with scorn and a certain regret, then he turned to his bodyguard. "Whereas you wait here. I'll have to deal with you later. I'll tan your hide . . . "

And he left the room in a hurry. In the large hall, before reaching the stairs, he thought he heard the telephone ringing. He dashed for the stairs and heard the telephone ringing clearly. As he was ascending he heard the ringing for a third time, then it stopped. It must have been ringing for quite a while and I did not hear it, he thought, slowing his steps. Hell, he swore. He went into his room on the upper floor and prostrated himself on the couch. He closed his eyes and his limbs were hugged by sweet exhaustion. The caretaker of the villa appeared again, crawling on the bed, with her eyes full of terror that made her look especially charming, made her look younger, and she started to sob and her sobbing turned to panting, now she was panting as if she had difficulty breathing or as if the weight of a male pressed her down while her plump chest heaved up and down, her firm flesh gleaming through her half unbuttoned chemise, begging to be torn open. Probably I was wrong to send her home, the minister thought, still imagining he summoned her to this room separately, ordered her to take off her skirt but keep her white apron that covered her belly and partially her thighs, while her wonderfully chubby buttocks under the straps of the apron kept swinging to and fro as this ripe experienced harem female danced under the eyes of the pasha, and he dashes for her and presses his belly on her firm fleshy chubby buttocks, he is tired, worn out, old, so he cannot get inside her, as the other one did before him, his younger and stronger bodyguard, and yet he does not feel ashamed and humiliated because he is more powerful than the other, he was able to grab this female still warm from his bed. Nonetheless he had not grabbed her for his personal exploitation, though it was tantamount to doing so because he thought that the point of all the severity with which he treated others was aimed at being able to do something while forbidding others to do the same. All their minds are set to one and the same thing he thought, and he was disgusted with himself as he compared himself with the others. I shall castrate everybody, he felt like screaming. And at that instant he saw himself through Ferhat's eyes, as if he already knew about his affair with Magda, this Ferhat who was the embodiment of chastity in matters of honor and was the only one who abstained from debauchery because he was impotent, he was not a man, he did not have the conquering male potency, which the bigger it is the more it drives you to the peaks of power, though he was considerably powerful yet craved and strove to become much more so, but to realize it he followed other pathways that suited his listlessness, he wanted to realize it but had not succeeded so far; slowly, unnoticeably, just like the drowsiness that creeps in gradually and once it enfolds you, it is very difficult, almost too late to shake it off without sleeping to the end the sleep which might be the last, but the Minister of the Interior had already understood his rival's intention and it was not too late, and though overpowered by a sweet slumber he shook it off, jumped to his feet, and rushed to the telephone to ask his man at the mental hospital if there were any tidings from the two isolated persons, the archive employee and the other lunatic who alleged he'd met Viktor Dragoti and insisted it was him and nobody else, when at that moment the telephone rang again and he woke up baffled, finding himself leaning on the couch, he had not budged and had not done anything and he thought for a moment it was Magda calling and he could not decide whether he had really called her before or dreamed he had, but as soon as he picked up the receiver he could recognize Doctor Basri's voice, his own man, who was calling from the madhouse at this hour to inform him of something extraordinary. At last.

"Speak louder," the minister said. "Are there any people around?"

"No, not in this room," the doctor replied. "But there are people in the hallway."

"Well, come on, raise your voice, nobody knows what we are talking about."

"As I was about to report," Basri went on, "following your orders, I locked up our friends in the same isolation room, under constant surveillance. And it yielded results . . . "

"Really? What . . . "

"One of them, the former Sigurimi officer, approached the other one and started to talk to him, telling him in detail what had happened to him this morning, how he met someone by the name of Viktor Dragoti who had died many years ago and had now risen from the dead, since otherwise it could not be him, how he had lunch with the resurrected, what they talked about, how he reported this to the branch head commissioner and so on and so forth, up to the moment they took him and brought him to the hospital. Unlike his previous babble, his speech was pretty clear and made sense, quite distinct like a normal person telling a story, only that occasionally he would skip something and mix his own story with the movie *The Adventures of Ulysses,* and he did this so eloquently you could say it was one and the same story . . . "

"Well, well," the minister cut him short. "Aside from this, was there anything else? How did the other one react? Did he speak?"

"This is what I wanted to expound upon, Comrade Minister," the doctor said in a self-important tone of voice. "At the beginning, Comrade Minister, the other one had the same affectless behavior, wrapped up in his silence as within a shell. No word, no movement, his eyes riveted. As if he did not hear anything, as if he were by himself. But when the nurse brought their dinner, he threw himself at the nurse's feet, grabbed him by his knees, and pleaded with him to be let out of that room, out of the sight of the other man, and to be given pen and paper, he had so many things to write about. Eventually, this is what took place. The other one, the former officer Qemal Daka, was so perplexed and horrified by all this that he totally lost control, and now it was him who shrieked and screamed at the top of his lungs at intervals, and there is nothing else interesting to be squeezed out of him, now I can say he is completely deranged. Unlike him, the other patient, Naun Gjika, is a special case and though he has a series of visible schizophrenic traits, apparently he is bringing out a few things that might interest you . . . "

"No need to make evaluations," the minister cut him short. "Hold your zeal and let me come to conclusions. You are only supposed to report, so tell me what Naun Gjika brought forth, what he wrote."

"At your orders," the doctor said. "Right now I'm going to summarize the contents of the long letter he addressed to me. First he declares that he is not Naun Gjika but the navel of the universe, the harbinger of God, and the Lord of the World of the Dead himself. From the time the Leader died," the doctor went on, lowering his voice, "because according to him . . . "

"What, what?" the minister screamed, and his teeth grated against the receiver. "Raise your voice, I can't hear you . . . "

"According to him, God forbid, the Leader is dead, Comrade Minister . . . "

"I got that, but raise your voice."

"At your orders. But farther down he writes that the Leader is immortal because he is God and has assigned him, that is, the scribe, through the Minister of the Interior, that is, through you, a very, very important task—the preservation of the files that hold the souls of all the enemies killed or executed or who died in prison or disappeared—and so for this reason he is the Lord of the World of the Dead, but later he confused himself with the Leader or says the Leader lives through him from the time he died. And he writes that since he guards the files in which the souls of those I told you about are locked, he is the master of those souls who are grieving to come back among us and mix with the lives of the living, but as they are inside the files, they cannot return because they cannot find the remains of their bodies spread as they are in unknown graves, because being souls locked in the files, they cannot read what is written in them, because they are chained to the written words. However, the patient goes on, from the time, God forbid, the Leader died, some of these files with the souls of the enemies have disappeared and been lost, by transcending, according to him, the threshold of existence and nonexistence which as it seems means the threshold that separates life from death, and have gone to hell, or Hades, where they are right now . . . "

"Where?" the minister asked.

"In hell, or Hades," the doctor repeated. "Hades, according to the ancient Greeks is hell, Comrade Minister. As it seems, he has borrowed this word from the prattles of the other patient about that movie, *Ulysses*. Apparently this word stirred Naun Gjika's brain and it brought forth this monologue. This is what happens on such occasions, a word suffices to release all the flow of thinking . . . "

"What else," the minister said, "does he say anything else about the files?"

"At your orders, Comrade Minister," the doctor said. "This is what I wanted to say. He writes that the files have gone beyond, to the other world; some of our enemies that were there have returned, they have crossed over to this side, and others will return, in exchange for the files that keep disappearing and being lost no one knows where and how, so little by little the world of the dead will swallow life in its entirety and both the living and the dead will be together."

"Oh, God," the minister let out. "What else? What else does he write about?"

"This is all, Comrade Minister," Basri said.

"Good," the minister said. "Very good. Where are the written pages?"

"They are right here, Comrade Minister, on the desk, right in front of my eyes."

"Good. Collect all the pages and come here urgently."

"At your orders."

"So. Quick . . . Wait, listen . . . I am not at the ministry, I am at the place we met last time. Do you remember the place, or do you want me to send my car?"

"Thank you very much, Comrade Minister, I remember the place very well. I have the emergency van here and I'll be there soon. I'm leaving right away."

"So much the better," the minister said. "See you."

He put down the receiver and then glanced at his watch. It was twenty-five minutes past eight. The doctor will be here in fifteen minutes, he said to himself and headed toward the stairs to wait for him in the entrance hall. There he found his bodyguard, sitting on a chair in a corner. The minister felt like screaming and insulting him for his shameful act but then he remembered it had happened in his dream and not for real, though he had seen in his bodyguard's face a certain expression of confusion, fear, and guilt, probably because he sensed his master was about to reprimand him, or it may have been, on the contrary—the minister thought about it seeing the expression in his bodyguard's face—that it was this expression that made the minister always find fault with him. But the minister had no time to be mad at him.

"Listen," he said, "Doctor Basri will be here soon. Go outside and wait for him in the front yard. As soon as he arrives, bring him in."

The bodyguard stepped out and the minister remained alone. He sat on one of the black leather armchairs opposite the door with his gaze fixed on it. He could hardly wait to see Basri with the papers written by the archive employee. Until he could lay a hand on them, he looked at his watch with the phosphorescent hands that showed on the black face. As if they had not moved at all. In the meantime his mind started to work feverishly. His thoughts were coming in swarms, jumbling and muddling with one another, contradicting one another, and he tried to put them in order and stay out of them. One of the two, he thought, either Viktor Dragoti was not killed or he is an impersonator. However, the next morning he had to issue an order for the arrest of several archive employees, starting with the director, he would arrest him himself. Because Viktor Dragoti's file had disappeared and its disappearance could not be unintentional. Several days ago this file was there, the director of the archive had admitted that he had seen the file with his own eyes. Its disappearance, however, and apparently the disappearance of other files, as Naun Gjika confessed, we will see to this matter as soon as possible, intended to cover up something or somebody, the fabricated death of somebody who was presumed dead and gone but who would reappear again later, just as Viktor Dragoti did, presumably the disappearance of his file meant that the unknown person who was becoming known now that they were chasing and would soon be apprehending him, the one who was becoming known, was Viktor Dragoti and nobody else. Hell yes. Of the two possibilities, this was more probable. You could even say the most probable. For as long as all those who met him thought it was him, then that meant it was him, even if it were not him, in which case he was him. And Ferhat, the perfidious traitor, could change nothing. Now, it was more impossible to pass the living for the dead than to bring the dead alive. Ferhat was cornered. All threads led to him, the Minister of the Interior said to himself. Those sinister invisible threads that can be found only through suppositions. When suppositions grow and multiply, the threads start to thicken and become ropes, ropes that can tie you up and not let you budge. And very rapidly, within five minutes, the rope will tie into a knot, as soon as he has the papers in his hands, which may prove finally and irrefutably with no room for doubt that the disappearance of the file or files was Ferhat's deed, that it was Ferhat who did it, because the saying that the files had gone through hell or Hades indicated that it was his name thus mentioned* and all the story of crazy Naun Gjika could not be expounded and explained but with the disappearance of the files and with the fear of those who had ordered this disappearance, or more precisely, of the one who had ordered it, and as it came out, it could not be otherwise, it came out it was Ferhat, because only someone as powerful as him could do this and only a power like his could intimidate to the point of madness and only in this way could all this gush of words from the lunatic be understood. So everything was crystal clear, the Minister of the Interior thought. Then he again recalled Viktor Dragoti's corpse washed by the waves on a deserted shore. Various pictures, alive and dead. Anthropometric measurements, the results of the experiment. Once more the minister realized he had started to believe that Viktor Dragoti had returned from the dead. Why not, he thought, why should there be somebody else? After all, it makes no difference who's who, nobody defines it but your file and in it quite a few things can be omitted and others can be added. Or the file can disappear and be lost, and then you are nobody or you can be anybody, neither dead nor alive, or both at once. A series of files had been lost, the minister thought, as he imagined a cluster of spirits clinging together in the form of wind vortices wandering in search of their bodies, their remains buried in undetectable graves, carried by the wind that blew and swirled in despair over barren land, over hills and reefs and precipitous river banks, but their search was futile, because the remains of those killed were so great in number and their burial places were so scattered, everywhere and nowhere, and from their burial and exhumation several times in different places and never by the same gravediggers, the special teams that took charge of the remains changed interminably and no gravedigger team was ever the last, the remains were continually displaced in remote places,

*Ferhat's name is a pun in Albanian: Fer (like ferr, meaning hell) and hat (like had, echoing "Hades").

under endless twilight, while the wind kept wailing and moaning over them, nobody knew where the remains of those killed were, they were always everywhere and nowhere and only the file of each one of them knew and only the ones who possessed the files had power over the life and death of each and every one. A series of other files are lost, the minister said to himself, but we already know and we will harness their spirits, because we will again get hold of the vanished files, or at least, we have those who have destroyed those files in our hands. After a few moments he would have those written papers, more valuable than any file, in his hands, because they would give him the key to the gates of hell or Hades, the key that would lock Ferhat up once and for all, and lo and behold! the headlights of a car flickered over the misty glass door and it was the emergency psychiatry van that brought the man with those written papers that the Minister of the Interior was waiting for so impatiently. The minister got up and dashed forward as his bodyguard opened the door and stepped aside to let in Doctor Basri, who, clad in white, resembled an angel and with a determined light gait made for the minister, while opening the doctor's bag he was holding in his right hand and with his left hand bringing out a bunch of papers folded in two, passing them from the left hand to the right and extending this right hand to the minister who grabbed the papers fearing lest at that very moment the papers would catch fire and turn to ashes between the fingers of the person who was handing them to him which he did at last.

"Very good," the minister said to the doctor and shook his hand. "You have done an excellent job, unquestionably."

"Thanks to your brilliant idea, Comrade Minister," the doctor said, smiling shyly. "To put them together in an isolation room."

"Yes, as if I knew it would come to this," the minister said, pleased with himself. "After all, you have done a great service to the government, which won't go unnoticed . . . Now you are free, go and have some rest, because you have already spent all your Saturday."

As soon as the doctor left, the Minister of the Interior went back to where he was sitting previously, waited until he heard the van leave, and then started skimming over the papers in his hands. He got the impression that at times the notes were very clear and transparent to the extent needed, and at other times confusing and incomplete to the extent needed, so that Ferhat, the archtraitor himself, and the other traitors identified thanks to his precise deductions and who were to be arrested, would clarify during interrogation, and he the Minister of the Interior would lead the investigations in person, and his findings would coincide infallibly and inevitably with the deductions of the Leader, and eventually the answers provided by the traitors during interrogations would inexorably coincide with those deductions, whatever they would be, sorted out by the farsightedness of the Leader, who would pave the way for the Minister of the Interior to the heights of power, as his secret forechosen successor, whose mind would coincide with that of the Leader in every step to be taken without the need for the Leader to speak explicitly, he could do it vaguely and ambiguously, because this is what suited him and this is how it had to be, thus whatever these presumptions, they would inevitably coincide with the occult and obscure meaning of some signs in the document the minister was holding in his hands right now, which had the power and strength of destiny so that everything would come out beautifully and smoothly from him and to his heart's content. So, said the captivated and enthusiastic Minister of the Interior to himself as he stood up and made for the door. His automobile was waiting for him outside. The bodyguard and the driver were strolling in the front yard. As soon as they saw their master, they rushed to the automobile, its headlights and engine started promptly, as the bodyguard waited like a statue, holding the handle of the open passenger door. The automobile made half a circle, then crawled out to the street, as the bodyguard closed the wrought-iron gate of the yard in a hurry and they drove on through successive bends and curves until they came to the broad straight street that connected to Martyrs of the Nation Boulevard.

"Home," the minister said, lost in his exultation.

He had to get some rest. Later, by midnight, he would go to one of his deputies, the one who was to be arrested in a few days, and there he would call his closest collaborators to draw up a plan of action to be carried out at dawn and during the entire day tomorrow. Now it was clear to him what he was going to do. It was like the Leader himself was inside him and directing him correctly in everything. In everything, really. The Leader was leading, while he, the Minister of the Interior, was nothing but an obedient somnambulist who implemented with the blind precision of fate some orders that had crept secretly into his brain. He took his briefcase from the seat, opened it, and put in the papers he was still holding in his hand when his fingertips touched a pair of sunglasses, a present from one of the deputy foreign ministers in charge of the Secret Service at the Ministry of Foreign Affairs, who was going to be arrested the next day. He squinted at his watch with the phosphorescent hands that glowed on the black face like two bones progressing through the night, coming closer invisibly but determinedly to a very anticipated moment. Then he put on his glasses and immersed himself in darkness. He kept them on though he could not see anything but darkness. He was blind. He was the Leader.

■ □ ■ □ ■

CHAPTER EIGHT

The moon was nowhere to be seen, nor was the sun; he would not be able to see the sun in his last day-night in this world . . .

AS HE REACHED THE DOORWAY, ALL OF A SUDDEN IT DAWNED UPON him that the woman might ask who he was from behind the door and he did not know how to respond. He wondered why he had not thought about an excuse for knocking on an unknown woman's door in the middle of the night, what to tell her when she showed at the door, since he was essentially a stranger to her. Sheer madness from top to bottom, he thought, still standing hesitantly at the door. And then what? Even if she recalled his face, this would change nothing. All this occurred to him only now, since a while ago he was overpowered by angst-ridden uncertainty as to whether he would find Ana's house again, whether she would still be there or had moved somewhere else, though his memory was not that of nine years ago but of nine days ago, and then he saw the light in her apartment and that very instant his heart started racing frantically and he felt as much alive as all other living beings, and since his heart was pounding like that it was impossible for him to have died before and the idea of his death was nothing but a weird nightmare, he darted up the stairs and his heart sank and anguish almost choked him as he thought the light could be a misperception of his senses, stupefied by the downpour of deliberations, until he reached the doorway and there he could not figure out what to do. Beyond that door could be either the fulfillment of his dream or utter nothingness, a sordid stark disenchantment at the moment of awakening and that creeping atrocious sensation of emptiness in which he would vanish with no return, and at that instant he experienced déjà vu, he felt he had gone through this pointless wait behind that door in the past and now everything was going to be repeated inevitably. But he had undertaken a journey beyond belief just for the sake of this dream and were he persistent enough to follow it through he would inevitably come to this door even if he could not hear the approaching footsteps climbing the stairs. Cutting his deliberations short, he knocked on the door, trying to make up an excuse, a fruitless excruciating effort under the circumstances, until the moment the door opened and a woman's disheveled head appeared, and it was Ana's. He recognized her. She seemed to have recognized him also, because without hesitation she flung the door open and without uttering a word beckoned him in.

"Welcome," she said at last, her voice sounding surprisingly affectionate and concerned at the same time.

Viktor Dragoti entered the anteroom and she quickly closed and bolted the door after him. She must have been at the concert or most likely she thinks they are after me, he thought, as he recalled Professor Dakli's words about how she offered him help heedless of the troubles that could have befallen her by doing that. Without asking any explanation from this late guest, as though his arrival was customary or anticipated, she ushered him into a narrow room, or so it seemed, overburdened as it was with furniture and other objects thrown helter-skelter. A dense bluish smoke floated in the air.

"This is where I live. How do you like it?" Ana curled her lips into a vague smile. "There is only one chair, as you can see, and I am the only one who sits on it, nobody ever sets foot in this place. But you'd better sit there . . . "

And she pointed to a sofa with a low tea table beside it laden with a couple of books and ashtrays, an open notebook, a cognac bottle, and a glass filled to the brim. She opened the window a little bit to let the smoke dissipate.

"Are you cold?" she asked Viktor.

"No," he said.

She left the window ajar and made for the door.

"Wait a minute, please," she said. She went to the kitchenette and returned with another glass, put it on the table near the bottle and went to the window to close it.

"It's a little untidy here," she said, bringing the chair closer to the table, and then she sat down. "But I feel better like this . . . Would you like some cognac?"

"Just a little bit," Viktor said.

"Well then, the big glass is for me and the small one is for you . . . "

She poured the cognac from the small glass into the big one, then took the bottle and filled half a glass for herself and one full for him.

"I drink a lot," she resumed. "What else can I do? Unfortunately I do not get drunk anymore. Once this helped me forget but little by little my body became accustomed to it and it has no effect on me any longer. I still keep on drinking though . . . this seems to me some sort of consolation, a necessary consolation . . . how can I explain it . . . "

As she spoke, she got up and took a cheap cigarette package from a shelf, offered it to Viktor who refused it, then sat again, and lit a cigarette for herself. She talked and talked, telling him how she had started drinking after her divorce, though the divorce was not the reason of her despair, it was something quite different, it was life itself that made her feel dejected and consumed and vexed all the time at everything deceitful that surrounded her, the divorce, no, she did not consider it a drama, but the end of a farce and as she kept talking Viktor kept staring intently at her face that had a faded likeness to what it was nine years ago, a face furrowed by time and distress. Only when she laughed did her face change for a second, it sparkled brighter and looked younger. What do I need here, Viktor thought, what business do I have with this woman, after all what can I tell her, can I tell her how much I loved her, or rather not her but her former exquisite apparition, that ethereal image or whatever. Though coming here, listening to her, and wanting to say something to her, no matter what, made no sense to him, still he sat there listening, not knowing how to get up and just leave or where to go, or probably he stayed there nailed by a vague curiosity for this woman, so unexpectedly close because of her queer behavior and so unexpectedly distant because of her withered charms gone forever with the wind, and he still sat there brooding in despair as if in anticipation of a miracle that could not happen, of a going back in time so that this woman would again be the one he had known before.

"We were divorced with no fight and no ill feelings." Ana went on with her story with an insatiable thirst for pouring her heart out to somebody, spilling out all she had suppressed within herself for so long because she had no one to whom to tell it. "He wanted to make our divorce look like a fight and destroy me, which he could have done since he had the power to do it, you know, with his circle of relatives and all that . . . Once, his uncle, the one who is a member of the Politburo, summoned me to his office, and you can imagine how he threatened me. But they did not succeed. Isn't it strange? Maybe God himself protected me." Ana's eyes widened, sparkling with a feverish light and her fixed gaze fell on her interlocutor, then she added with a cool smile, "I divorced him because I simply did not love him. The truth is I never loved him in the first place and of course I made a mistake by getting engaged. I still feel ashamed of myself when I think I accepted marrying him because I was mystified by the grandeur and pomposity of his powerful circle. Then this feeling grew to disgust for the man, because he always bragged about his circle, which for me became more and more intolerable. I separated with no pain, but in the meantime I had contracted a loathing not only for him but also for everything I come across that I consider unbearable, such as lies and self-debasement and mortification of ordinary people in the face of power. Do you understand me?"

"Yes, I do," Viktor said.

"Probably because I found myself in that situation, I can see it now in everybody and everywhere. And maybe you'd say I overdo it a little. But this is how I feel and with the passage of time instead of fading away this feeling has become stronger because I see that lies and self-debasement are growing. Consequently I try to shun people, stay behind closed doors, live in seclusion, but this is impossible. I love my profession and I find solace in it, a kind of relief, though every battle against cancer is unrewarding. But cancer patients are more truthful than other people, especially when they understand what their disease is. Occasionally they may become worse, more wicked and nasty, but even then they are more truthful, because they are stripped of lies and appear as they are, what they have inside comes to the surface, in the way the scanner penetrates and reveals all body organs down to the skeleton. The same thing happens to cancer patients and their loved ones and families. And I feel relieved when I alleviate their pain.

Being close to them makes me more sensitive to the big lie that creeps into the lives of other people."

She raised the glass and drank it to the full.

"Aren't you keeping me company?" she asked Viktor.

He raised his glass, hardly touching his lips. In the meantime, Ana filled her glass again. Such a downfall, Viktor thought, overpowered by her words, such an unyielding self-destructive tendency. But seemingly an individual can enjoy freedom in this country only in this fashion. The liberty of this woman was almost awe inspiring.

"What about you?" she asked suddenly. "Tell me something about yourself."

"Your engagement was the reason I decided to defect," Viktor began, astounded at the same time that he could express himself as though resuming a broken conversation. "Or rather because this engagement, at least as I imagined it, had a certain connection to the power, it was the power that was separating you from me."

He stopped an instant, lost for words. What am I talking about? he thought. But it was already too late. Ana was staring at him, not looking surprised at all.

"So I decided to disappear. My disappearance was more than an absconding. Perhaps I was willing to die without realizing it. I left at night, swam in the direction of a cluster of lights flickering in the distance, a foreign ship offshore. It was too far away, and the farther I swam the farther the lights seemed to be. I doubt if I could have made it even if the coast guard hadn't spotted me in the meantime. But as I told you, I had already decided to disappear in one way or another. I was almost absolutely sure they'd kill me. It was a moonless night and I was surrounded by waters as dark as the sky above and death itself. Suddenly I was flooded by a blinding light. It is coming, I thought, this is it. It was as though I was waiting for it, as though I knew beforehand that this would be the end. I was also pretty sure that they would not make any effort to capture me alive, they'd simply kill me in cold blood. They started to shoot from afar, as the coast guard was closing in on me with only one headlight on, resembling the Cyclops's single eye, fixed on me. At the beginning I could not tell whether it was the roaring of the coast guard boat or the volley of guns. It is impossible, I said to myself, though I already knew it could not be otherwise. And yet I was not dying, as machine guns crackled more deafeningly and the boat engine resounded more loudly. Then I plunged into darkness, but I was not yet dead, I had only dived in a futile effort to avoid bullets, because after an instant I buoyed again on the water's surface and the dazzling light and the hot metal pierced my body in tandem and all this kept recurring as though it would continue till the end of time . . . "

He dragged his story through so much detail in an effort to delay telling her the unspeakable, but he did not know how to avoid it.

"So they killed you," Ana butted in.

"Yes," he said, and he stopped, not knowing what else to say.

"Then," Ana picked up, "then you went to a dreadful location, from which no one has ever returned and there you stayed for nine days, though for us nine years passed by. Then you came back."

"I came for you," he fumbled.

"I've known since then that you loved me. I have always loved you, too. I have always waited for you."

She had bent forward, her face close to his. Viktor stretched out and threw his arm round her shoulders and brought her closer to himself. They kissed for a long time. He felt his cheeks wet with tears he knew were not his. Ana was weeping silently and between kisses stared at him, smitten, and smiled with a smile dolorous and sensual at the same time, as her body attracted him as it did once, and as he touched it he could feel it open up gradually and her face also changed, or was it that he had already got used to it by staring at her all this time together, or was it that little by little, during this endless and yet brief time, her face infatuated him again, anyhow either this woman was one and the same with the one nine years or nine days ago, or not a flicker of time had passed by. Viktor Dragoti could not determine whether everything was happening for real or whether he was in a dream, he got the same dreamlike impression he had been having quite a few times during that very long day, which could dissipate then and there, yet he had remained within the dream of his journey to here, to this woman he was undressing hastily, fearing that the dream could come to an abrupt end, and as she let him undress her without uttering a word and without taking her enamored eyes off his body, her hands undressed him hastily, and he, diffident, feared he would be unable to make love to this woman, and she, understanding his diffidence, started to caress his body ecstatically and he again immersed into his dream, not thinking about whether he was in a dream or out of it and then they yielded to one another vigorously, and again after that moment he could not tell whether he was still in a dream looking at her naked exhausted body lying beside his, not even when he felt he was waking up and she was still there close to him as nine days or nine years ago and all their lives forever and ever, as time had come to a standstill, and they made love again in ecstasy, then dozed off again, and again woke up to give everything to one another to the last drop through the endless night, through love and dream, and he realized he had longed for this woman and this dream in his life and beyond his life and beyond his death, the entire flow of his life and the journey of his death had aimed at this, the flow of a moment replicated endlessly during that night, when he united with this woman and this dream, in which he perceived time with no beginning and no end, compressed in one single instant and his destiny in the form of a huge oak tree, whose crown swayed in the wind as the leaves whispered the words of his ballad and his life, which was the story of a dead man whose life was a narration recounted by this oak tree, as the mirrored crown of roots went deeper and deeper into the depths of the black soil as in death and into the body of this female to reach the dark source of life and the blinding light of that moment when life and death intertwine, which is the beginning and the end of everything, just as both their dreams intertwined with one another and she saw the enormous oak of her destiny, with the roots deep into the womb of the earth, that sucked up relentlessly within its depths as dark as the abyss of hell his living trunk full of veins, as the crown of the oak discharged the blinding lightning of a prolonged moment that aimed at eternity, she would wake up and pull him toward her body and her smooth belly seeking to unite with the crown of the oak tree to the dome of the sky, inviting and swallowing the storm and the lightning and the potency of his veins to the dark source where life begins within her, again and again, realizing that her destiny was to love this man then and from now on and the rest of her life she'd continue to live only for her longing for him and for the moment of a crazy love cut off so painfully during the night of all nights, whose end was drawing near and he had to go, he could not stay any longer, the miracle was impossible beyond that first and last night, he had to leave before dawn, because there was a ship waiting for him somewhere between the sea and death, he had to hurry through the margin of life and death and through the narrow boundary between day and night, he had to run, and she saw him through the window running through the street as the black-lacquered carriage stopped before him to carry him to the seashore and to the brink of death, the black carriage with lowered black curtains that soared in the dark sky and the river of clouds that took him to the grayish waters of the sea, and he lay both dead and not dead, as the current brought him up to the black veiled ship anchored in wait for its primordial and last sailor to take him to the end of his last journey.

CHAPTER NINE

Both dead and not dead . . .

THE PRINCE OF THE UNDERWORLD, LORD OF DARKNESS AND THE
world of the dead, was languishing in one of the innumerable pits of
his cavern. He did not know, nor had he ever known, whether he
could not see because he was blind or because of the darkness, in which
case were he not blind he would not be able to see anyway. Perhaps he
had singled out this obscure haven as immense as the darkness itself
quite by chance, from the very beginning, from time immemorial,
solely to forget that he was blind and not from any craving to become
lord of darkness, a very tedious job from which he derived no satisfaction whatsoever, as he might have presaged unconsciously even then
at the beginning of time. Or perchance, he could not ascertain, he had
indeed craved to become what he already was, because apparently his
will and his being were one and the same thing and because seemingly
he could not crave to be anything else but what he already was, the
Prince of the Underworld and lord of darkness and the world of the
dead, merely because he was blind. Because, being in darkness, even if
he had eyes that could see he would not be able to see anything, so being in the same darkness where even all the other spirits, ruled by his
eternal malediction as they were, though they had eyes that could see,
roamed blindly in the darkest darkness of this cavern, which was his
domain, in the darkness within darkness, as was the fathomless funnel
that opened up somewhere into this cavern, growing perpetually
deeper and deeper and darker and darker, and there, cursed from
birth, toiled the maledicts ignorant of why they were born and yet

born to die, thus being in this darkness, the sightless lord of this darkness and the Prince of the Underworld would forget his blindness. He would not be able to recall that somewhere out there was light and everybody, dead or alive, slave or omnipotent master of all slaves, yearned for it. As a matter of fact he did not know how and what it was, but prying as he did into the grief-ridden spirits agonizing at the bottom of the funnel he had overheard and grasped somehow from their stories that light must be something that belonged to the other world, and, as they said, it was emitted from some sources such as the sun and the moon and fire and flowing waters and lightning, and even people emitted light, they bequeathed and received the light of that blinding instance, in which converged all the light emitted from these sources, they had such a craving for it, the fools, and more than anything else, for the dazzling moment of copulation between man and woman when they created a new life which was at the same time the beginning of all lives, and those fools feigned not to know, though they knew too well, it commenced to expire in the eternal darkness of death. Anyhow, the Prince of the Underworld and the lord of this darkness of the dead, of their death and resurrection, could not imagine how and what light was, how things would look if his single eye, whether opened or closed it made no difference, could see. His wish could not but coincide with what he was and with what happened to him, with his endless weariness caused by the recurrence of the same events over and over again in his realm, the world of darkness and death, because apparently it had been prophesied, as written in a book, which was the book of all worlds, that everything that took place was related to a story in that book written no one knew how or why or for whom, but with the purpose that things must never change for anybody, though nobody could read that book, because everybody was within it, thus establishing once and for all that he, the Prince of the Underworld, lord of darkness and the world of the dead, hence lord of all worlds because everybody was headed toward death and everything was under its supreme authority, this almighty god, therefore, would be concurrently and simply and purely for this, the slave of his own endless weariness, so that he could be powerful enough to satiate his every single wish and have no desire to shake off his weariness. And to suffer and agonize and grieve merely for being incapable of wishing to be otherwise and to be otherwise his wish could not be powerful enough to accomplish. He went through interminable agony and torment and weariness, languishing for eternity in one of the innumerable alcoves of his cavern, with the longing for something very cherished and forever lost, yet not being able to visualize what it was, possibly because he had never had it, because had he ever seen the light at some point, he would have dreamed of it in his dreams, as they say the blind who have not always been so do, but could not perceive whether he was dreaming or was within a perpetual dream, as he was constantly in a state between being asleep and awake, in a dream-wakefulness state, which he had the vague feeling of coming out of occasionally, as though a little while ago he had been somewhere else he could not recall where, and now, this instant, he was experiencing the feeling of being awakened, just as never before or maybe just as very many times before, though it had always been impossible for him to recall, even now he could not see a thing, only his ear could perceive something like the rustling of the feathers of a bird seemingly flying out of the realm of darkness and of the dead to once again return among the living, something that could not happen, it could not come from his great black birds, his servants were ruled out as they could only see in the darkness of this cavern but not outside it, therefore he concentrated to find out what this feather ruffling was that seemed to be going in the direction of the world beyond, and he pondered, as in a dream within a dream, what that could be, until it dawned upon him that it was the shuffling of papers flying in the air, soaring high to get out of there, a bunch of written papers, which had descended ahead of time in exchange for someone who was leaving with his permission, that of the Prince of the Underworld and the Lord of the World of the Dead, and it was Ago Ymeri's spirit that had been allowed to return among the living for a single day. And now this errant spirit was returning to the abyss of the realm of shadows in exchange for these departing written papers that held the key to that spirit, so that it remained eternally within the obscure abyss, because all that happened to a human being in his previous life and the curse that followed him in his afterlife in the darkness of the cave of death was contained in that book he could not read and consequently not change, because he was within it, he was shackled inside it, so neither could he know nor could he understand anything from the spirit's previous life, whose each and every event was meshed and interlocked with another event and a myriad of other events before they had ever happened and before they ended, just as in the afterlife beyond death his book would always be unreachable, always beyond, on the other side. When his spirit was in the world of darkness his book was in the world of the living and if he were ever to return among the living for a single day for as long as the lord of darkness and the world of the dead would allow, then the book that had the secret of his enslavement and whose slave he was would cross over to the world of darkness, in the underworld realm of shadows, where he was held prisoner, but when he returned again to this side, that very instant the book would cross to the other side beyond, there to the world of the living. Why should this happen, since by crossing over the book that has the key to the spirit of one of my slaves becomes inaccessible not only to him but also to me, he brooded despondently, and then he vaguely brought to his mind a distant dream, in which those written papers had disappeared, while a missing person, whose enchanted reflection they were, had reappeared and now was disappearing again, becoming twice as nonexistent because for a second time they were killing this being who had become nonexistent nine years or nine days and nine nights ago. At this very moment the enchanted mirror of his file was reappearing in its place in the secret archives so that he would continue to be missing, just as in an exchange with its disappeared person, replacing him in the world of darkness as ransom for his return at the right moment foreseen by the lord of this world of darkness who this very moment when the missing file was being exchanged for the missing person, one crossing to this side and the other to that, was transitioning from dreaming to wakefulness, or perhaps from wakefulness to dreaming, he could not tell, because he could not see anything whether dreaming or awake, blind as he was everywhere, in this world and down yonder, and he could not distinguish now which world was his, because the wakefulness of one world was the dream of the other, he always forgot afterward, and only now at this very moment he was realizing who he was in the other dream world, which was always the other one, incomprehensible for his mind, just as this world was the other one for that world, so he did not know in which one of them he was, maybe he was in both simultaneously, both lord of this and of that, and in this very moment when the twice-missing person was being killed for the second time, as he swam toward a boat he could never reach, after being brought to shore at dawn in a vehicle ordered for the purpose by the Minister of the Interior, who had come there in person to follow closely the entire event to be replicated just as it took place nine years ago, but adding some detail it lacked then, i.e., the presence of the Minister of the Interior, this was the reason why it had to be repeated, just as he had been instructed by the Leader himself, just as he could recall from a distant dream he had forgotten until then, a blind dream he had never seen but had only heard of, and it rang in his ears as the echo of a primeval story conceived in time immemorial, the story of a book about a world he had once been in and that was his dream at the same time. The Minister of the Interior, however, would carry out the order of his Leader to the letter, because he was his Minister of the Interior, his servant, obedient and zealous, because it was fear and terror that made him such, in spite of how things appeared, because there was no loyalty and no trust but fear, the terror he felt lest the Leader were to dismiss and exterminate him, crush his head, as he had crushed the heads of many before him, made him obedient. So head crushing will continue, in a dizzy dance of heads that gnaw at one another and invite and bring other heads in this dance, in the vortex swirling within a blind eye, whose darkness devours voraciously, endlessly, because I can never be obedient to the blind loyalty of someone else, because this is only the end result of that unheard of terror I mentioned, so for that reason the Minister of the Interior carried out the order to the letter and because he carried out that order to annihilate a missing person and the one who would be his successor, if he, the Minister of the Interior, though he would not be, he could not be, were to be annihilated and sucked in by the vortex of the dance, the trap he had set up himself, each one of my possible successors would disappear into the same trap they set up for one another and themselves by obeying me, they have to be eliminated, because they have a little too much power, yes, so that no one will have my power, after I am no more, thus the successor to the Leader must be someone with not too much power, someone who even after the death of the Leader will remain under the power of his shadow extending over him from the world of the dead, and now these two have to be purged and together with them many more, and none of the survivors should become so powerful as to extend the shadow of the dead Leader over the heads of the others, because there should be someone who could be identified with his shadow and be his shadow, hence above everybody else, so that he could have power over all others like the petrified and immortal reflection of the Leader, so that he could be his shadow, but in this way it could also happen that this shadow could detach itself from the one who cast that shadow from the world of the dead, identifying itself with the omnipotent he would have left behind, the shadow of his shadow could abandon him and join the other one, whose head would stick out after the death of the Leader, just as that of the Leader had stuck out above all other heads, therefore the number of those to be gobbled up and devoured by the ever-growing vortex in the darkness of its blind eye, which was the unfathomable darkness of the realm of the dead, and this vortex kept expanding incessantly, and the more he felt his death drawing near the greater the number of the heads of his successors that whirled and swirled and then were sucked up inside. Now a telephone was ringing informing him that a man who had died nine years or nine days and nine nights ago had been killed once again and he was dying, and that his Minister of the Interior had made his last step toward the abyss by carrying out the order of the Leader to the letter though he understood where this order would lead, which were he to disobey he would again step over the abyss, because the order was such, a black abyss his servant could not steer clear of, whatever he did, so better obey oh you servant loyally to the end, so as at least to believe that you delay your terror but only in your mind, for as long as you can, and feel like you are eating the head of someone else and forgetting that that head is both his head and your head at the same time, because you my servant can never possibly be my successor, because after you there will always be another head that will eat up your head which in turn will be eaten by another one, until no head survives to become my image as perpetually immortalized and untouchable as both my power and my shadow, that is why these authoritative heads with mangled jaws are crushed and gobbled up in the monstrous mouths of one another, an abyss within an abyss within the blind eye of the world of darkness, while the black cord of a telephone goes down and down through the underground, deep down and on the way up comes through it the echo of a dream that recounts events that have not taken place yet but will, he now imagines what this dream from the world of the dead foretells, something he could not see even if he were not blind, because it will take place after his death, the dream foretells how the spirits of the dead, the ones he killed, will return at one point in time, but those who will return in search of their corpses in unmarked graves will not be the servants he exterminated but his fierce enemies because they hated him with their frightening hatred, as the meek, voiceless scream of his fear called on them to return, he imagined their exhumed bones, thousands upon thousands of skeleton trees that sprang from the earth everywhere, dangling and crackling their phosphorescent branches that glowed horribly, as a steamy nimbus rose from them and covered everything and wiped out your shadow from the surface of the earth, because your enemies hated you so perniciously they could not be kept under leash in the world of the dead any longer, after your death, because you had to reign over the world of the living to have the dead under your leash, and reign you should in the world of the dead to keep the living under leash, because you had to be on this and that side simultaneously, but after your death there would be no one who would be an omnipotent god, because only one could be such, and that one was only himself, all the other servants who could become like him if he were to let them would be devoured by the blind and irresistible vortex of darkness that kept swirling, that neither he nor they nor anybody else could restrain, and thus the vault of the world of the dead would rupture and he would no longer be the master after his death and while dying he would wake up from the dream he was dreaming while alive of himself being the god of the world of darkness and the dead, because he would no longer be the god of this world either because he would not exist any more and would have left no one who could protect his shadow, the vault of his underworld cavern would split open and from its chasms and gorges the spirits of his fierce and hated enemies who abhorred him so fiercely would flow forth, the spirits of those who were killed or had disappeared in prisons and nameless graves and enchanted secret files, full of incantations to keep their spirits away, who would return no matter what, as the return of a single dead man had portended, which the Leader would exploit to get rid of some of his servants who might take his place after his death, as if in this way he could put off his own death, because he was blind to see the doomsday the return of the dead portended, the one he had allowed to return as he had heard his nostalgic lamentation that made him miss the loss of his sight which he might have never had and consequently had never been able to see, that is why he was full of envy, a regurgitation of hatred for all that pertained to the world of the living, so much so that this hatred that gurgled from within, within his darkness and from within the depths of his world of darkness filled him up and turned mysteriously against him, the dome of his underworld vault smashed to smithereens and the world on this and that side melted into one, the living were over-flowed by the river of those killed by him, those cursed and lost spirits who were nevertheless being resurrected now, at the time the clock with two hands of huge bones indicated by shining dazzlingly on the dark dome of the sky and the bones of volatile arms were shattered and scattered into a dazzling light as their dust adorned the firma-ment, from whence the bright cascade made of the bones of countless skeletons fell rumbling down overflowing his deserted cavern where he twisted and turned painfully in his eternal loneliness. He was com-pletely awakened by a dolorous twitch, which almost suffocated him, and it dawned upon him he was nowhere else but in his bed, though he was still in the grip of a remote and vague feeling that he had been somewhere else a while ago or was living another life, but all this was a dream he had forgotten already. The twitch was almost gone at the moment of his awakening but the feeling he had from the dream still lingered on, tormenting him, something impossible as much as it was horrible, and upon awakening he felt he could not see anything but darkness since he was dead. I do not see because I am blind, he thought, trying to soothe himself. I only dream of dreams my mind fails to re-member. This is how he woke up every morning and every time he thought this it was an evil omen. But then, as he plunged into the day-to-day work he had always accomplished successfully and would con-tinue to accomplish, he was more and more convinced that death would never come upon him.

■ □ ■ □ ■

ABOUT THE AUTHOR

BASHKIM SHEHU was born in Tirana in 1955. He has written about the last months in the life of his father, Mehmet Shehu, who served as second-in-command to Enver Hoxha during the Communist regime of Albania. After his father's death in 1981 under mysterious circumstances, the author and his family were persecuted, and he served part of a lengthy jail sentence before the democratization of Albania. He has lived in Barcelona since 1997.

■ □ ■ □ ■

WRITINGS FROM AN UNBOUND EUROPE

For a complete list of titles, see the Writings from an Unbound Europe Web site at www.nupress.northwestern.edu/ue.

Words Are Something Else
DAVID ALBAHARI

Perverzion
YURI ANDRUKHOVYCH

The Second Book
MUHAREM BAZDULJ

The Grand Prize and Other Stories
DANIELA CRĂSNARU

Peltse and Pentameron
VOLODYMYR DIBROVA

Balkan Beauty, Balkan Blood: Modern Albanian Short Stories
EDITED BY ROBERT ELSIE

The Tango Player
CHRISTOPH HEIN

Mocking Desire
DRAGO JANČAR

A Land the Size of Binoculars
IGOR KLEKH

Balkan Blues: Writing Out of Yugoslavia
EDITED BY JOANNA LABON

Fire on Water: Porgess and The Abyss
ARNOŠT LUSTIG

The Loss
VLADIMIR MAKANIN

Compulsory Happiness
NORMAN MANEA

Border State
TÕNU ÕNNEPALU

How to Quiet a Vampire: A Sotie
BORISLAV PEKIĆ

A Voice: Selected Poems
ANZHELINA POLONSKAYA

Estonian Short Stories
EDITED BY KAJAR PRUUL AND DARLENE REDDAWAY

The Third Shore: Women's Fiction from East Central Europe
EDITED BY AGATA SCHWARTZ AND LUISE VON FLOTOW

Death and the Dervish
The Fortress
MEŠA SELIMOVIĆ

The Last Journey of Ago Ymeri
BASHKIM SHEHU

Conversation with Spinoza: A Cobweb Novel
GOCE SMILEVSKI

House of Day, House of Night
OLGA TOKARCZUK

Materada
FULVIO TOMIZZA

Shamara and Other Stories
SVETLANA VASILENKO

Lodgers
NENAD VELIČKOVIĆ